For JJ, my number one person.

xxx

While some scenarios are inspired by personal events, the names and characters in this novel are fictional. Resemblance to actual persons is coincidental.

Contents

Green Curry, Lady! 1

Miss Moneypenny, I Presume..............................13

Growing Pains 23

Lonely Cat Ladies...37

All The Single Ladies...51

Everything Is Completely Normal! 59

Potsy 67

Number One Person 73

Bye-Bye, D 79

The Hip Bone's Connected To The... 89

Personal Independence.......................................101

He Can't Help Being Called Kevin.....................111

Who's She? 117

The Power Of Facebook......................................123

Everybody Needs Good Neighbours 131

The Fog Has Lifted 137

Magic Hands 143

All Too Familiar 151

Pain In The Bum 157

Speculate To Accumulate 161

Life's A Beach 165

A Nice Problem To Have 173

Sunday, Sunday Here Again, Tidy Attire 177

The Sunny Side 185

Epilogue 195

Bonus Chapter 197

About The Writer 205

Why The Zebra? 207

For Anybody Who's Interested, ...208

Dedications 209

Chapter 1

Green Curry, Lady!

Christ on a bike, I'm down again!

My eyes gradually focussed on a dusty old copper pipe behind the sink. Noticing the green patina around the welded joints, I could see from where I was lying on the grey-and-white Victorian floor tiles that this place hadn't been cleaned in a *pretty* long time.

I lifted my head slightly, noticing the beginnings of a tender bruise developing on my left cheekbone...

I'm pretty sure I wasn't imagining the black patent kitten-heeled shoe right in front of my face, attached to a pair of slightly stumpy legs which were straddling my head...

Huh?

I started to feel the faint-sweats coming on again - my ears were ringing and my vision was closing in, so with only the bright shine from the patent shoe still in focus I decided to rest my cheek back down on the cool floor tiles.

Ouch, but ooohhhh, the cold felt quite nice actually.

The owner of the shiniest shoes I'd ever seen (who was thankfully wearing jeans and not a skirt, otherwise the view from where I was lying would have been much worse), stepped away from applying her lip gloss in the gilded mirror, and without uttering a word she pulled open the heavy door and walked back out into the restaurant.

Only in London would you get such an accomplished *'nothing to see here'* attitude from a perfect stranger!

I wasn't sure how long I'd been *relaxing*, but I knew I was having trouble coming out of this one. I managed to shift slightly, untwisting the wrist trapped awkwardly underneath me, just in time to go back to the land of nod for another fucked up few minutes.

In and out of my dream-like state, I was trying to piece together what had brought me here. Not in a soul-searching way, I literally mean *'Where The Fuck Am I?'*

You think I was pissed, don't you? That I was some kind of lush who couldn't handle my Negroni?

Nope, not a drop.

We'd stopped for lunch in a little Thai place we'd found down a side road near Oxford Street. We were on a non-date, as we'd called it to take the pressure off, when I'd suddenly reached a firm 8 on the *Faint Scale*. They call this 'pre-syncope', but I don't just go out like a light - I usually get a slow build-up, so I go with my 0-10 scale.

Chances are if I get to an 8 I'm *going down.*

I remembered telling Potential Boyfriend *'I feel a bit funny'* just in time for him to catch me from falling face first onto the table (*I imagine my eyes would've stung like holy bugger if I'd fallen into my tofu green curry - all that chili!*).

I'd come around pretty quickly and decided to try and walk it off, so I'd gone to the loo to splash some cold water on my face.

Only, I was to discover that this was not a one-off drama, it was a mini-series and I was now on about episode 3, I think.

I had no choice but to lie there waiting for it to pass. I knew from past experience that getting up too soon was utter madness and was how things like broken bones happened. *'Better to lie down than to fall down'* was my mantra, no matter how inconvenient the location.

I thought I might've just finished the final episode when I came around again in the company of two lovely lady paramedics, who were hunched over me in the small space between the sinks in the ladies loo, slightly out of breath from lugging their gear up the steep staircase. Potential Boyfriend (PB) had come to find me when I didn't come back from the loo FORTY MINUTES ago!

Oops.

After tentatively poking his head around the door to the ladies he must've been a bit concerned to find me crashed out on the floor, poor thing. Anyway, understandably I suppose, he'd called 999. Given that I'd passed out at the table it was fair to assume there was something amiss.

It's a good job his concern was reasonably warranted - imagine if your date went hunting after you for taking your time over a stubborn poo!

It has to be said that no thanks *at all* were due to the patent shoes/stumpy legs lady who hadn't bothered to check if I needed any help. I was wondering what she'd thought I was doing there, spread-eagle on the tiled floor, dribbling into my hair.

Maybe she'd thought I was the cleaner seeing to the dust on the copper pipes and was having a little rest, bemoaning my lazy arse to the rest of her table over dessert.

I could've been in a diabetic coma!

Seriously, where did this woman usually hang out that she was so used to finding people crashed out on the toilet floor at mid-day that she'd casually straddled the haphazard heap to get closer to the mirror and perfect her peachy pout? Wouldn't you at least be mildly curious?

I guess she just assumed I was *'on something'*...

As I was pondering all of this, the lovely ladies in green had decided that my heart rate and blood pressure weren't behaving, and they ought to take me in. By now I was coming around enough to start paying attention, so I noticed when they gave each other a pained look at the thought of lugging me down the staircase of the converted Victorian property, now a thankfully quiet - *if suddenly nauseatingly fragrant* - restaurant.

'Can you walk, love?' the older one asked, with a hint of hope in her voice.

'Yes, I think so.'

With surprisingly strong hands placed under my armpits (dear god I hope I'm not sweating too much!) the two kindly ladies propped me up on either side until I was gently laid down on the narrow bed in the ambulance.

This would in fact be my second trip inside one of these bad boys, although I have no memory of the first trip in my teens.

While they attached a few wires, muttering something about *arrhythmia* and *hypotension* to each other, they were asking stunned Potential Boyfriend questions he clearly had no answer to, when there was a knock at the back door of the ambulance.

Who the holy hell knocks on the door of an ambulance?

With a loaded pause, clearly expecting abuse from a shouty-angry Uber driver who had been inconveniently blocked in (which according to the Daily Mail was a growing problem for our poor paramedics these days), the pretty blonde one (surely she's not old enough to be out of school yet?) nervously opened the back door to find a petite Thai lady holding aloft a brown take-away bag repeating *'green curry, green curry lady!'*

You couldn't make it up.

We refused the impractical green curry that I'd lost the appetite for (I think PB had eaten his Pad Thai while I was occupied and he had access to cutlery), which might've been a godsend for me because I'd started to wonder - if the loos were that unclean maybe the kitchen wasn't in the best state either.

After what must've been a much shorter ride than it felt like, where I'd drifted in and out of a dream that I was on a Mediterranean cruise, rather than rattling about in the back of a van (it feels more like being kidnapped!), we were safely delivered to the rather busy Royal Chelsea Hospital for the rest of our non-date.

There began the usual round of tests, only this time they added a new and unexpected one.

'You're not pregnant, Lizzy, and it is not the *menopause.'*

A strongly-accented and obviously knackered Doctor had delivered the news.

I could've bloody well told him that, if he'd bothered to ask!

Three things:

1) I've been single for so long that if I was pregnant they'd have to write another Bible.

2) Pregnancy and menopause are not ideal subjects to discuss on a first non-date - how embarrassing!

3) Thank Fuck for that!

I mean, I knew it was *impossible* that I'd be pregnant, and I was pretty sure I was too young for the change, but hearing it said out loud was still a bloody relief, all things considered. A few other standard test results were delivered over the next couple of hours and when they could find no reason for my current drama I was sent home to rest and told to visit my GP 'soon'.

'Ha! Have you tried getting a GP appointment these days?' remained unsaid, of course.

'It was so bloody embarrassing! I haven't fainted like that for ages, but trust me to make a fool of myself at a time like that. Can you imagine what PB thought?'

I was relaying my latest drama to the girls. Kay's eyes were sparkling in that *'trying not to wet herself laughing'* way she gets when attempting to keep a straight face.

Kay and Elle were school-gate friends. I'd known them a few years since our little ones had started school the same year and we'd become great buddies. We were all quite different really, but when we weren't moaning about the men in (or in my case *out of*) our lives, we were usually having a hoot about some nonsense over coffee and cake. Usually on Friday lunchtimes, as we tried our best to keep our much-needed weekly therapy date. As a single, knackered, working mum I needed this all the more, and they'd also turned out to be awesome stand-by lifts for Charlie if I was late for the school run (and vice versa, of course).

'What happened after they sent you home?' Elle, the more practical of the two women was more in control of her giggle reflex than Kay was.

'He got me as far as Waterloo Station and put me on the next train home. Thank Christ I got a seat, I was like the living dead I was so zonked out afterwards. I'm not sure I even said goodbye!'

Shaking out my painful wrist, having obviously aggravated an old fracture that never healed properly, I went on 'I don't reckon I'll be hearing from PB again, do you?'

I mostly directed this comment at Kay who'd been the one to push me into this adventure - so convinced she was that he was The One just because he'd sent me flowers for my birthday last year.

'Course you will you numpty, you're so *nice!* Why wouldn't he want to see you again?'

◆

Now, let's pause here a minute. I know there are a lot of people who would wince at being called nice. Don't worry - I'm not one of those people. I am nice. And I'm not being boasty - I am definitely not a boasty person. But there are a lot of things that I am not: (beautiful, vivacious, dynamic, athletic, energetic, exciting… you get the picture) so I am very happy with *nice.* And as I've got older and met some really nasty shits along the way, I have come to realise that I am *properly* nice. It's always seemed perfectly natural to me and it's come as a shock more than once in my life to discover that not everybody is!

I'm the one who notices when somebody is poorly and needs some TLC, turning up with supplies of Lemsip and tissues; the one who walks to the shops to get milk for my neighbour when we can't get our cars off the drive in the winter.

And I always see the best in people - I'm not one of those women who'd slap down other women they feel threatened by. I don't make a song and dance about it, I'm a very quiet person, but by nature I am a cheerleader.

A *nice* friend.

It has taken me a long time to acknowledge that I have a positive trait, and I am really not good at accepting any kind of compliment, even one as generic as *nice*, but I have finally come to accept that this is my thing. I don't even mind *too nice*, which crops up quite a lot!

And we're back in the room...

◆

Elle was agreeing with Kay by now. We didn't always agree with each other and we weren't sycophantic, but on this point they both stood firm.

'You've been 'chatting' for a few years now - there's no way he'll drop you over this, even if you didn't come clean about your *predisposition*,' Elle said, with one eyebrow cocked to emphasise her point.

A few days later they were proved right, when PB messaged me to check I was OK.

'Yes, fine thank you.' I actually felt my cheeks go red at the awful memory of what I'd put him through.

'You gave me a bit of a fright!' he replied, obviously hoping for more from me on the subject.

'I'm so sorry about that, but it's nothing to worry about. I was just a bit dehydrated, I think.'

We rather awkwardly passed the time of day for a while until he gamely asked if we could see each other again *(Kay will wet herself!)* and I agreed that the next child-free weekend I had, we'd give it a go. I wanted to think about it, really, and I knew this bought me some time at least.

Ok, so I hadn't warned the poor fella before we met up. I didn't go around telling everyone about my randomly-occurring health problems - why would I when the medical profession kept telling me I didn't have any?!

Besides, we all know when we're asked *'hey, how are you?'* that people don't really want to know.

It is absolutely standard to say *'yeah good thanks'*.

I only told Kay and Elle after I'd known them for at least a year, and only then because I'd ducked out of two consecutive Friday lunches and I'd wanted them to know it wasn't personal.

I was just feeling like a bag of shite and couldn't get myself out of bed. I was embarrassed to bring up something so personal, but they took it well. *'Bloody hell woman, why didn't you tell us before?!'* and *'you look so well though, you'd never know!'* were the general responses.

The truth is I either looked pretty well, or I looked like I'd been exhumed, but if I knew I was going out I could pull it together enough to make sure I didn't scare children and animals.

I didn't go on to all and sundry about how I felt, not just because there's nothing worse than seeing somebody's eyes glaze over in utter boredom, but also because I knew nobody could understand what it was like unless they'd lived it. I mean, I was much healthier in my 20s - working full time as a Marketing Manager (pre-Charlie) and after a long day followed by a full-on spin class, or sometimes 'power' yoga where I impressed the teacher with my uncanny ability to get into the most bendy positions, I went home saying I was *pretty* tired.

So I know it's absolutely IMPOSSIBLE to explain to people what the type of tired I live with these days feels like - the words just haven't been invented. And when you know that everyone is thinking *'yeah yeah, we are all tired, Lizzy'* it's just uncomfortable to try.

Because it's true, *everyone is tired.*

Everybody works hard and has responsibilities - I would never diminish anybody else's problems. But besides the random blackouts, having lived the 'healthy' kind of tired back in the day, I have to say the relentless malaise and fatigue I feel these days seems very, um... *unhealthy.*

In the old days after a full-on gym session I'd rest for an hour or so and be back at it, but these days if I change my duvet cover I'm out for the rest of the weekend.

I put on a bloody good show so nobody would know, which helps me to live as normally as possible. It may not sound like it, but I actually am a bright-side kinda girl. So, I didn't bring up my predisposition for fainting, the fact that I am always knackered, or the fact that various bits of me are always hurting...

The girls said I should tell PB before we met up, but I didn't want sympathy or judgement, and I was convinced that bringing it up with him would lead to one or the other.

Nobody at work knows either and I've been working at the school for a few years now. Well, not counting my boss and the chap I share an office with, who had to know in case he needed to lie me down and hold my legs in the air if I passed out.

He's very happily married and a bit of a Gent so he went quite pale at the thought that this man-handling might ever be necessary. Particularly since the #metoo campaign is gaining momentum and poor well-meaning blokes are being disciplined at work for such things as innocently remarking on a female colleague's new haircut. It's all so confusing for the average non-sex-pest, so I promised I would always wear trousers to work just in case.

So no, I don't talk about myself much. I really don't want to be known as either: 'You know, Lizzy - the poorly one?' *(Shame isn't it? She's so nice!),* or equally as awful, the not poorly one who just complains a lot. (*I can't see anything wrong with her but she's always moaning about being tired and shit. We're all bloody tired!'*).

So it generally didn't come up unless absolutely necessary.

But Fuck Me Dead, I should have predicted that I'd have a bad day when I least wanted to, having finally agreed to this non-date with PB on a rare child-free weekend.

Chapter 2

Miss Moneypenny, I Presume

I met PB in the strangest way - I'm almost embarrassed to tell you! Born in the 1970s, I'm not really from the online generation, but when I'd split up from Charlie's dad after our long and mostly happy marriage accidentally fizzled out when we weren't looking, I'd found myself awake at 2 am wondering what the hell I had to do with this Form E that my solicitor had sent me.

I'd sat up and grabbed my cranky old laptop and with it overheating from sinking into the duvet, I'd Googled it - as you do. Before very long I'd found myself joining a divorce *forum*.

Yes, really.

The web page said, 'We provide all the resources you need to get through divorce' *what joy*, and I set about reading the lengthy legal advice pages. Before long, a bit overwhelmed by all the solicitor-speak, I'd found myself snooping on the much more interesting chat window in the sidebar.

Members didn't use their real names of course, and you could tell a lot about their state of mind from the username they signed up with: *'Innocence'* clearly thought she'd done nothing to deserve being dumped, and *'ShesAGreedyBitch'* was more than a little angry about demands for spousal maintenance.

Their real-life dramas took my mind off this bloody Form E, which I still hadn't really looked at, and I'd found myself snooping the next night too.

These people were clearly going through the same nocturnal stages of divorce that I was, since they were all logged in after hours, and it was kind of reassuring to know I wasn't alone.

Everybody had a different tale of woe, with one poor woman having the police on standby because her ex was stalking her in a very disturbing way *(what drama!)*.

Anyway, there I was minding everyone else's business, when I saw my username mentioned in the chat window.

Shit.

For some reason I held my breath for a full minute (something someone prone to fainting really shouldn't do) as 'Spiderman' called me up on being nosy and not joining in. Apparently, this is poor form in a chat room.

Fuck, I actually didn't know anybody could see me hanging out here...

So, as Miss Moneypenny (don't ask) I had to make a decision. Should I stay, or should I go now? I guess the biggest decision about my relationship status was already made, otherwise I wouldn't be hanging out in G-Vorce, so you'd think deciding whether to stay or leave a bloody chat room would have been relatively simple...

Spiderman: 'hey Miss Moneypenny, don't be shy!' *(smiley emoji)*.

Innocence: 'she's been in the group a few nights now, has anybody seen her chat?'

Feeling Blue: 'do you think it's one of our exes spying on us?' *(This was the lady with the police on standby - I guess that'll make a person paranoid).*

Christ alive, what do I do? Why do I feel like I've been caught with binoculars pointing at my neighbour's bedroom window? Not that I know what that's like, I don't even own binoculars, but you know what I mean.

Remembering to breathe out before I fainted, I decided to answer. I was brought up with good manners, after all, and the last thing Feeling Blue needed was to worry about another stalker.

Miss Moneypenny: 'hi'

Innocence: 'Hi!!!!' *(waving emoji, I think, I haven't got my reading glasses on).*

A few others added to the welcomes, with varying degrees of interest and even more exclamation marks.

Miss Moneypenny: 'Sorry, I wasn't meaning to be nosy. I've never been in a chat room before and I was shy about joining in! I'm new to this whole divorce business *(I'd soon find out how much of a Business it really was)* so I didn't have any advice to offer anybody. Sorry, but I was really just here looking for information about my Form E!'

I hit 'send' but then decided I should have added a smiley face emoji to make sure they knew I came in peace, so I sent one afterwards.

Spiderman: 'Pleased to meet you Miss Moneypenny, sorry to hear you're getting divorced too. It sucks! Me and Innocence have been around here for a while and can help you sort out your Form E if you like?'

And so it went on. Night after night I'd found myself cross-legged on my bed in the early hours, chatting to virtual strangers while my son slept in the adjacent room.

I'd even started to settle down with a glass of wine before logging in, but I was mostly still snooping to be fair. Most of the others had much more interesting stories than my 'we grew apart' tale, but I was also getting just enough off my chest to make myself feel a bit better.

It was sooo much easier than talking to people who cared about me, so they wouldn't worry about how bad I was really feeling at the demise of my long marriage.

It was true that I'd never done any kind of *online* chat thing. I mean, I use computers for work, banking and shopping of course, but I've never entered the realms of online chat.

I'd met Charlie's dad when I was still in my teens - this was before the invention of The Internet, let alone the nightmare of today's speed-rejection sites like Tinder.

I admit I was starting to like the anonymity of the whole Miss Moneypenny thing, and when 'MrD' (I'll come back to why I nicknamed him this later) started to get a bit friendlier I'd quite enjoyed the distraction.

After about a month we'd started to PM (personal message, I learned) so we didn't have to sit in a group chat getting to know each other while Spiderman repeated an upsetting story about his ex-wife making child access arrangements difficult. It was clearly causing him heartache and he brought it up every time a new member joined the group.

It turned out he was a member of Dads Need Justice and I'm sure it was him climbing on the roof of his local Tesco Express on the news the other day, waving a sign made out of a single bedsheet and highlighting the plight of estranged fathers. It was all rather brave and dramatic, spoiled only (in my opinion) by the comedic value of a skinny grown man wearing a Spiderman outfit.

Anyway, it turned out that PMing MrD was my first mistake as a single adult. After a while he'd started messaging way too often and he began saying things like '*I feel so close to you,*' and '*I think about you all the time.*'

I didn't take it personally at first, after all I was just words on a screen and not a real person to him, but I was starting to get a bit cautious and was making doubly sure I didn't lead him on. More than that though, it was becoming a bit tedious, truth be known. He'd started to be a bit needy, expecting me to answer his messages for hours on end, and frankly I had enough on my plate without feeling responsible for somebody else's happiness.

One evening he sent me a link to a song (probably after too many wines) called 'You're Everything,' by an American rock band I'd never heard of.

With lyrics professing:

'You are the strength that keeps me walking
You are the hope that keeps me trusting
You are the life to my soul
You are my purpose
You're everything'

My initial reaction was *'Got over the ex a bit fast, eh* mate?'

It was a nice enough song, but holy hell that was uncalled for!

Actually, if you're looking for a wedding song give it a listen, I'd say it's a close second to Tom Baxter's 'Better'.

He'd asked for my home address soon after this, and it was all feeling properly sketchy by then, so I ignored the question and began making myself scarce. I mean, I'm not stupid - and clearly by now alarm bells were ringing louder than my pre-faint *tinnitus.*

Not sharing my address turned out to be a good call, as he later told me why he'd wanted it.

You're thinking flowers, right?

Chocolates? Wine, maybe?

Nope. You will NEVER guess.

It turned out he'd made me a model of his Actual Dick.

Apparently you can buy a kit to mould your own erection!? He'd made one to send to me in the post to see if we *fitted together!*

W.T.A.F!

He even went into detail about having to shave his bits so the latex wouldn't stick! I shut him down before he attempted to explain how he'd maintained his, errr, *position* while the thing set...

So yeah, MrD (named after his Dick-moulding kit of course) was the first man I'd blocked from my newly-discovered online world.

Ohhhhh, you thought I was going to say that was Potential Boyfriend? *Good lord, no!*

PB was the poor sod who had to work a hundred times harder after this madness, firstly to prove he'd never model me a dildo from his own erection to send me in the post, before I would let my barriers down again.

We ended up being virtual buddies for a few years before we actually got around to meeting up. Partly because we lived in different parts of the country, but also because I was pretty reluctant to start something I didn't really have the time or energy for.

He was signed up to a few dating sites and over the last year or so he'd asked for advice over Skype about what to wear *(not the pink shirt again!!)*, that kind of thing, but nothing had worked out for him so far. We were getting on pretty well so we decided to meet up to see if the comfortable chat on messenger worked in real life too.

But it was *definitely not* a date...

By this time the divorce was truly done and dusted, which was actually pretty sad, and me and Charlie's dad had sold our nice four-bed detached house and split the equity.

We'd been in a hurry to grow up, for reasons I'm no longer clear about, and we'd got our first mortgage when we were just 19 years old. Much as that been a huge burden during our early 20s, it had paid off eventually and we had a reasonable pot of pennies to share.

He'd moved to London for a fancy new job and I'd bought a new little place just big enough for me and Charlie, about a mile from the sea in a quiet East Devon town.

◆

Much as it was pretty devastating to lose everything we'd worked hard for and start all over again, I liked the family who'd put an offer on our house and they'd seemed really excited to move in.

However, in another demonstration of how shit my experience with men was, the bloke turned out to be a bit of a stalker. He was buying the house with his wife and little girl, who looked to me about 2 years old, and as the sale was progressing there seemed reason to pass on contact details...

Well, he started getting *in touch.*

At first it was quite easy to believe it was all normal, under the circumstances. 'I was wondering if I could pop by and measure the garage so I can get my shelving ordered,' had seemed fine.

'Of course!'

I'd let him into the garage and he'd carefully measured the space, explaining that he was a bit of a neat-freak and would have it fitted out with custom shelving.

Dull, but whatever floats your boat I guess.

And you probably know that when you sell a house you can make a list of things you'd be willing to sell direct to the buyer should they want them - things that are not attached to the house *(like, you wouldn't list the loo)* but things like a shelf unit that fitted perfectly into an alcove. He'd asked to come around and look at some of the bits on my list, and afterwards he sent me a message.

'Thanks for letting me come and look at the furniture today. I'd like to buy the hall table please - you have good taste. By the way, you were looking very hot!'

I'd felt this was an odd thing to say, but the comment was just ambiguous enough that there was a small chance he was referring to the unusually hot day, so it was hard to reply *'Fuck off you pervert!'*

Another time it was, 'My wife was wondering if I could come by and measure the bedroom windows so she can get the curtains made?'

'No problem.'

I mean you want to keep your buyer happy, right? Only, I later got more text messages, including the non-ambiguous, 'Thanks for letting me follow you upstairs, your arse looked fantastic.'

Sweet Jeeeezus why do I attract the nutters?

One evening, having already measured everything and with no excuses left to ask to come in, I noticed his car parked up outside the house - not directly outside the front door but close enough to freak me out a bit. So I made sure my curtains were always closed before I got undressed in case he was loitering somewhere.

I mean the bloke had a wife, and a little kid, and he knew that I knew this, and I knew that he knew that I knew this - what the hell did he think would come from this behaviour?

After I'd moved out and the house was all theirs I assumed that would be the end of it, but he got in touch to say he'd received some post addressed to me and said he'd drop it over. He knocked on the door to hand over the precious post - *it was obviously bloody junk mail!*

It was quite a relief that I was staying with mum for a couple of months while my new-build house was being finished off, and the next time he came over (without asking) we saw his car pull up so I hid in the dining room and mum opened the front door. She told him I'd moved out and said if ever there was more post (I'd redirected my mail but sometimes the odd straggler would arrive at the old house) that he could drop it through her letterbox and she'd pass it on - *but if it was bloody junk mail to just bin it!*

Freak.

So, having encountered some weirdos since finding myself single (and a few while I was still married if I'm being honest) I was still cautious about PB being a potential weirdo/stalker/axe murderer, but I did think he'd have got bored of me if that was his thing, and would've probably met someone more inclined to accept the risk by now.

And after all this time, I'd repaid PB his patience by showing him my best underwear on our non-date.

Oh yes, apparently my dress rode up in the ambulance…

Chapter 3

Growing Pains

It was dawning on me that one of these days I should explain to Charlie what to do if I fainted, or had some other clumsy accident (pretty likely knowing me) when we were on our own, so that he wouldn't freak out. Or maybe he'd just ignore me and keep playing on his Wii, I'm not sure!

I'd thought I could get away without worrying him, but he really did need to know how to use the phone and tell somebody our new address now it was just the two of us. Not that fainting usually caused severe injury, and I did always put the knives blade-down into the dishwasher just in case...

He'd be my little saviour - one of those child heroes given an award by Carol Vorderman on ITV. Maybe he'd get a hug from his idol while they played his 999 call recording to the live audience.

Who would his idol be, I wonder, Super Mario?

◆

Let me give you some context... we need to go back a bit, ok?

I started fainting quite a lot just before my teens. I had a morning paper round from age 11 ½ - you were supposed to be 13 I think, but in those days nobody checked or cared.

I wanted to be able to afford to shop at Miss Selfridge and not just Paraphernalia (the second-hand shop up the road) so I really wanted this little job, but I'd kept passing out while I was waiting for my newspapers to be counted out in the cramped little shop.

I think the owners assumed I just wasn't bothering to have breakfast because it was so early, and they'd lectured me about this every time it happened while loading me up with the paper bag that weighed more than I did. They were mostly worried about the papers being late, I think.

Mum took me to the Doctors, of course. I was sent to our local hospital and tested for epilepsy, and maybe a few other things I can't recall, but every test came back normal.

It was *just a phase*, they said.

Mum made soothing noises but was probably pacifying me, safe in the knowledge that there was nothing actually wrong, having done her due diligence and getting me checked out.

A few years before this I'd been crying about pains in my legs but after checking it wasn't juvenile arthritis they said it was just growing pains.

To be honest we can go right back to me being born blue, and not in a Royal sense, but having come out with the cord wrapped around my neck I'd needed a little encouragement to start breathing. Trust me to be bloody awkward.

I was a slightly underweight baby with my dad's reddish hair and so-pale-it-was-translucent skin, which later developed freckles.

As far as I know I was OK though, until as a toddler I had whooping cough - the real nasty kind hardly heard of these days thanks to vaccinations, and I'd coughed so hard I'd burst both my eardrums. Apparently I freaked out my uncle by coughing until I was blue while sat on his lap one day - he kept his distance for a while after that.

This resulted in a few years of embarrassment as I was regularly called out of class to have my hearing tested by someone who came into school with all kinds of equipment especially, as the scarring on my ears drums had made me a bit hard of hearing. I managed just fine once I got over my little *speech impediment* (because I'd heard S as Sh and mum got concerned when I asked for shaushagesh for tea).

Dodgy ears was an ongoing issue, with mum regularly being called to collect me with raging earache a feature of my primary school years.

Back in those days mum worked as a receptionist at a Doctors' surgery and she would often just have a quick word, rather than book me in to see my own GP. I'd come out in a horribly sore, itchy rash one day when we were at the park and she'd whipped me into the surgery, just a few minutes' walk away, for them to have a look.

'You're allergic to the sun,' the nurse told me, 'you'll always have to wear sun-block in the summer.'

Great.

On another day I'd had a problem with my neck - I'd just woken up with it hurting like bugger, and the Doctor that my mum most liked (I think she had a crush on him, but this will always remain unspoken!) said I had *torticollis*.

Maybe I'd slept funny, or pulled something doing cartwheels, so they gave me a soft collar to wear for a while. This problem never really went away either and I just kind of accepted it.

If I said something was hurting, mum would say *'you've probably got bruised bones,'* as if giving it a name would make me feel better about the whole thing. It was only much later in life I realised there was no such thing as *bruised bones* - nicely played, mum!

There were other classic lines too, unconcerned as she was.

'Mum, it hurts when I do this.'

'Don't do it then,' she'd say.

So I was skinny and pale with what my dad had called 'lucky legs' - he'd said they were so skinny I was lucky they held me up. Mum tells me I was always happy though.

I prefer not to think I was feeble, but rather that I was 'dainty', and I'd considered myself to be a little ballerina. I think I'd got the idea from my musical jewellery box that had a little ballerina figure spinning around to tinny music when you opened the lid.

(I even wrote to Jim'll Fix It to ask if I could meet Margot Fonteyn and dance a duet with her - who knew the heart-breaking disappointment of that letter going unanswered would turn out to be such a lucky break! To anyone reading this who hasn't heard, 'Jim' turned out to be a right perv...).

I recall standing in fifth position during our ballet lessons and wondering why everyone else went all wobbly, sticking their tongues out while trying to force their little pink ballet shoes into the correct position when mine went like that so easily! I went to ballet classes for a couple of years until I'd got upset about being told off for not understanding the French words the teacher bellowed at us. I was forever being chastised for copying my neighbour instead, an older girl who went on to train at the Royal Ballet School.

'Grandes battements en croix. Eyes FRONT Lizzy!!'

I mean c'mon, I was only about six.

I think I was mostly in it for the tutu anyway, which I'd got to wear on stage for our seasonal performance at the local theatre. I was Spring. I even got to wear make-up which I'd thought was amazing, even if it was mostly green.

The trouble was I'd got so scared of the strict teacher that in the end I'd cried every time we got to the class, and since this involved mum getting a babysitter for my sister, two bus rides each way, and of course the long nights of sewing chiffon onto my costumes, she didn't fight me over it and I dropped out.

Shy as I was (I still am) I'd absolutely loved dancing. Our poor dad had to put up with the weekly Top of the Pops front-room-disco that me and my sister took so seriously that all the furniture had to be pushed to the edge of the room to make space.

I was generally *gymnasticsy*, too - one of my party tricks had been contorting and dislocating my joints *for fun!* It didn't hurt, and remember we didn't have iPads for entertainment in those days.

Looking back I think dancing was a coping mechanism. I'm not being all heavy about having to deal with a terrible upbringing - everything was fine. I just mean that I struggled to stand still, and dancing around must've helped. When it was my turn to do the dishes my legs used to end up looking like leftover corned beef - all reddish-purple, blotchy and itchy. If I danced around by the sink this didn't happen so much. I never really thought about why.

I was clumsier than most kids and I remember mum would despair at the times I got myself covered in mud or grass stains from falling over. I was in my best dress ready for a ballet exam one day and I'd gone to prance around the front garden to show it off to our elderly neighbours.

'Be careful of that dress, Lizzy, you don't want to ruin it,' mum had called out, and of course I got a grass cut on my finger and got big fat blood spots on the white cotton.

Sorry mum.

As I grew up, with many and varied illnesses, injuries and complaints (and a handful of scars - I really hated the one that made me look like I had a bit of eyebrow missing. I was hardly *Gangsta* so I didn't really pull off the look), all seemingly unconnected and with no medical explanation - everyone had me down as a hypercondriac.

I mean, fair enough, right? If the Doctors couldn't find anything actually wrong after blood tests, CT scans and X Rays, then maybe I was!?

I guess part of being a hypercondriac is that you don't know you are one?

So, I've just paused to google hypercondriac. This is the first explanation that came up (on Hypercondriac.org):

What is the meaning of Hypercondriac?

You might have first bumped into a hypercondriac when you attended school, but you wouldn't see them often as they would always be getting sent home early due to some mysterious illness you didn't think sounded plausible.

Their mum would then take them to visit the doctor because she was concerned about their health, and they would get the all clear after being checked over from head to toe.

That would usually only be the beginning of their illness, and the day after their all clear they would complain about more mysterious symptoms even though they looked perfectly fine.

I mean, I can't deny it - from the outside this is exactly how I looked when I was growing up. The way that I *didn't* fit that profile though was that I was never especially worried. Hypercondriacs usually fear serious illness, imagine their symptoms, or worry that trivial symptoms might suggest something more terminal. Essentially it's more of an anxiety disorder.

Nobody else would be able to see the difference, but I knew I'd never had that fear. I mean, I complained when something hurt, but I never argued with the explanation.

I always accepted that it was nothing to worry about and from then on I put up with it without further complaint.

By the time I was a teenager I thought life was this tough on everyone - not knowing that living with constant pain was just my own version of normal.

Although nobody ever called me a hypercondriac to my face, I think it was the first thought my GP had whenever I made an appointment. In a shit twist of fate I got glandular fever when I was 16, a month or so after my dad died (he was only 49 - he'd been poorly for a while so it wasn't a complete shock).

I was in a bad way and a slightly older boy I was hanging out with at the time - who *almost* became a boyfriend - insisted I made an appointment and drove me to the surgery in his dad's car. Due to the shit timing the Doctor said I was just grieving and sent me away saying it would *take time.*

Of course I was, but I also felt pretty sure that grief didn't make people feel like *that.*

After a few weeks of feeling really fucking shitty and hardly being able to get food inside me, I was down to about 6 stone and looking really feeble.

I admit that it probably didn't help that I had the whole Goth look going on at the time - I was studying art and design and thought I was being original. Yes I had blue hair, too....

Anyway, the lad I was hanging out with continued to be remarkably attentive for a young man, and took me back to the Doctor saying he was worried about me. (Don't think badly of mum - we didn't have a car so she couldn't get me there...)

This time they gave me a blood test (just to shut me up I think), but when I went back for the results it showed I had the Glandular Fever, or Mono/Epstein-Barr virus, and I was finally given antibiotics. I was off my feet for a couple of months - probably not helped by the delay in being treated.

I remember that when the test results came back the receptionist had said, *'Oh well, you can always re-sit your exams,'* and wondering why she would think I might need to. It didn't even occur to me that grief, illness and time off my courses might make me fail, I was so used to gritting my teeth and getting on with things no matter what.

Anyway I scraped passes in the end, somehow.

Go me.

We didn't become a 'thing' in the end. I'm not sure if it was because he thought he'd given me the kissing disease and felt bad, or if he was scared he'd get it from me, but either way this was my first relationship near-miss. While I was laid up he checked in on me now and then, but I wasn't up to going to Timepiece (the alternative club in town that we'd started to go to with a few of the art college gang) and he met someone else there.

She was a smart-suited trainee accountant by day and a glamorous, vampish Goth by night - and I couldn't live up to that.

Shame really, and not just because his dad was a bit loaded and let us borrow his Jag - which was definitely preferable to walking everywhere.

It maybe sounds like this must've been a shit old time, but I have fond memories of the good bits.

I confess I looked him up on Facebook recently. He's doing well for himself, living in Hong Kong with a fancy job and a pretty wife, so that's nice to see.

Like me, he grew out of the Goth look.

◆

I met Charlie's dad a year or so later. My friend fancied his friend so we'd go and nonchalantly dance near them at the club, until eventually we got talking and started hanging out. Looking back I can see that we were just kids, but it wasn't long at all before I left home so we could move in together.

Mum said she didn't approve because we were too young, but really it made it easier for her to go ahead and downsize now she was on her own. She moved into a nice little flat - it only had one bedroom though, so there was no going back!

Charlie's dad was already living on his own in a bedsit when we met, having fallen out with his mum he'd left home the day he took his final O Level (these preceded GCSEs, for those not ancient enough to have heard of O Levels and CSEs). His bedsit was spotless, but the rest of the men-only shared house was a bit of a dive, so we moved into a small, newly converted barn on the edge of a small farm.

Sounds nice, huh? You can almost picture an idyllic little Grand Designs type barn conversion set in the Devon countryside.

It was actually shit.

They'd done a terrible DIY conversion and the place was damp and bloody freezing. Money was seriously tight because Charlie's dad was still a trainee for the company that had taken him on straight from school, and I was still at Art College with just a Saturday job at the big supermarket in town, but we managed.

I was working 10-hour shifts on the checkout, which earned me a nice case of Carpal Tunnel syndrome so they moved me to the stuffy cash office, which was a shame as it separated me from the rest of the student workforce and it had been a bit of a laugh. But it *was* better for my buggered wrist.

Soon after we moved in we went to register with our new GP, who obviously took his cue from my old Doctor's notes and he kicked things off by saying, 'They probably never treated your depression properly,' and made me take a suicide-risk survey.

Holy mother of god, here we go again.

I mean, I guess I was a bit down sometimes, but only because nobody would believe there was anything other than 'being sad' wrong with me. Failing to get this across in my 10-minute appointments I'd sometimes cry (in frustration!), firming up their belief that I was actually *Very Sad Indeed.*

I suppose it's a bit like when somebody royally pisses you off then they have the nerve to say *'don't be stroppy!'* and you snap back *'I'm not being stroppy!'* leading them to smirk triumphantly back at you.

There's no way to win those conversations.

So my new Doctor gave me antidepressants, which frankly made me feel worse, since I was not, in fact - sad. At least, not about 97% of the time.

It was at this point that I pretty much gave up making appointments for anything other than smear tests and holiday jabs - stuff I thought they could handle.

I mostly hid the fact that I was often in pain, or felt like shit, because Charlie's dad was understandably getting fed up with it. He'd roll his eyes and say, *'You're the only person I know who can go to bed and wake up injured,'* which was actually a pretty reasonable complaint on his part.

I'd ruin things too... As we grew in our careers we actually started to be able to afford foreign holidays! But they were typically ruined by me having to lie down in the air con after about the second day, when my sun allergy (which I knew by now was called Polymorphic Light Eruption) kicked in and the horrible painful hives would sprout all over my skin.

Always the optimist, I was certain that the new ridiculously expensive, high factor, anti-allergy sun cream I'd bought this time would work, but nothing ever did. I kept to the shade, but still the difference between the UV in Devon and the UV abroad was too much and my skin just wouldn't cope.

I toured Pompeii looking like a Japanese tourist, walking around under my black and white spotty umbrella, which we'd actually taken in case of rain as the forecast had said we might get downpours.

(Not that I have anything negative to say about Japanese tourists, just that my behaviour looked undeniably odd for a Brit abroad).

Of course the fainting never quite went away either and it always showed itself at the worst times. After we'd been together for just over a decade we decided that since we'd made it that long, we may as well get married. Well, the day came around and you know that magical moment when the bridal car pulls up and the radiant bride emerges - all beaming smiles - and everybody gasps at how lovely she looks for her special day?

Ha! Not me.

I'd got out of the car a shaking, pale, sweaty mess and grabbed his hand saying, *'Don't let me go!'*

They sat us down for the ceremony (it was in a register office) so I'd got through it, but it was a really hot day and I'd totally struggled. We'd planned a nice, relaxed wedding and I did feel a bit better after a sit down in the shade and a few gulps of Pimms, so we got through the photos and speeches OK.

Traditionally, newly-wed couples might nip off for an hour or so to, well, you know…. And we went back to our hotel room between the wedding breakfast and the evening do…

…where I promptly fell asleep.

It's a wonder he didn't annul the marriage there and then to be fair, I mean we still had no idea why this kept happening to me...

'When I die and they find some bizarre illness at my autopsy I want you to put 'I told you I was ill' on my gravestone,' I used to jest to Charlie's dad. Except Spike Milligan stole my line when he died in 2002 so I can't use that one any more.

Chapter 4

Lonely Cat Ladies

So - present day, and post-divorce, home is now a little seaside town with a pebble beach, where I'd downsized to a brand new two-bedroomed house with Charlie and our obese little dog Lillie.

For some reason our house was rendered in a shit-brown colour, when all the others were either plain brick or neutral cream, but it's ours and I love it. You can't see the colour from inside, anyway.

When we bought the house the builders hadn't quite finished the inside, so I took the chance to request some changes which would make life a little bit easier. Since standing by the sink to wash dishes was *still* a problem, I decided to use the washing machine space in the kitchen for a dishwasher instead. I then asked them to change the plumbing upstairs and they brought pipes from the bathroom, across the hall, and into the large cupboard on the landing so I could pop a washing machine in there.

I know, as my dad used to say, *'not even a pretty face'*...

Not only did this little shuffle-around give me the useful dishwasher space I needed, even though the kitchen was *really* tiny, it also meant I didn't have to lug the heavy laundry basket up and down the stairs.

I had the lawns taken up too, so I could avoid the weekly task of grass cutting. I'd always quite liked gardening, but it wasn't the best of use of my energy these days.

Yeah, you can throw problems at me if you want, life, but I'll work around them! I reckon I'm still winning!!

The house may not be flashy, and it's pretty small compared to our old house, but I enjoyed being able to buy furniture and decorate it to my taste, without having to compromise with anybody. Charlie chose the colours for his room, but honestly he didn't give a shit what I did to the rest of the house. So, when I wanted to paint my rooms 50 shades of grey, so I did!

(I was really loving the current Scandi-inspired trend, you see. Plenty of Hygge - whatever that means).

◆

So here I am, middle-aged and single for the first time since I was 17. I'm no longer skinny so I've shaken off the Thin Lizzy label that followed me around for my first three decades. The main downside of this is that I can no longer share clothes with my sister. We used to swap things so we always had more wardrobe options, but these days I wouldn't squeeze into our old size 8s. At a diminutive 5ft 2" (and a bit) I often used to be compared to Kylie, but nobody made that comparison once I reached a size 12. I can't say I enjoy being bigger, but my sister pretends she's jealous of my new curvy figure to try to make me feel better.

'You're *voluptuous*, which is what men find more attractive. And you've got great boobs these days!' she said.

I suppose I didn't mind the boobs - at least since they're quite new they haven't started to sag yet...

I'm no beauty, but I like to think I'm just on the right side of normal. I discovered hair dye in my late 20s, so once my childhood auburn hair turned dead-mouse brown, I went blonde. Over the years I've nurtured a growing colony of freckles, but I can't say they ever worried me. I mean, I got teased over them at school so I didn't exactly love them back then, but these days I didn't notice them unless someone passed comment (actually you'd be surprised how often that still happens). To be fair I'd believed they had faded with age, until I got my first pair of reading glasses a couple of years ago and realised it was my vision that had faded and not, in fact, the freckles.

I have to say that being single is completely fine by me, except that everybody is pushing me to *get back out there* and I can't stand constantly disappointing them.

'You'll end up a lonely old cat lady crocheting blankets for premature babies and never leaving the house!' said Elle.

I think she genuinely worried about this, maybe because she'd given herself a head-start by actually getting the cats. She wasn't at all sure about her current relationship, *'He's a lazy git!'* she'd complain. But she wouldn't kick him out because she didn't like the dark and she said she'd be too scared on her own at night.

She'd gone ahead and got the cats ready though, just in case.

Relaxing at home on my own and having loads of time for hobbies actually sounded quite heavenly, to be fair, and I began to reel off the usual lines about being perfectly content in my own company. I didn't mention that I'd given up crocheting baby blankets because my hands hurt like bugger the last time I made one.

'I'm not miserably single, I'm *determinedly* single! With everything else going on I really can't be bothered to start back at the beginning of a relationship. It would take somebody VERY special to break up what me and Charlie have - we're a good team and we don't need anybody else. Besides, I honestly don't think I've ever been happier!' I said.

And this really was true. I know people always think being single is really sad, and that every single person is just pining the days away waiting for somebody to sweep them off their feet and make their life complete. But I really wasn't.

At first I was distracted by the practicalities of sorting me and Charlie out somewhere to live, the busyness of which helped me to get over the sad stage of divorce. Then once I was used to the idea of being single, I actually learned something about myself.

I'm a *people-pleaser.*

I've always put making other people happy above all else, which at the time made me feel wanted and needed. I'm not a bloody martyr or anything, if anything it's more self-serving really because seeing other people happy makes me happy, especially if I think I might've played a part in that. It's like it gives me purpose - so I matter.

However, when a people-pleaser puts that kind of pressure on themselves, it's quite upsetting when people are not that pleased after all.

Trying very hard - and failing - at making somebody else happy doesn't do much for a person's self-esteem, and for a person who already feels like a bit of a failure (thanks to the whole 'hypercondria' thing), it can be quite devastating!

Having realised this about myself, I acknowledged how much more relaxed I was without that self-inflicted pressure. I mean, kids love their parents no matter what so I was onto a winner with Charlie, but I realised that not having anybody else to please was actually really rather relaxing.

Not having anybody to apologise to when I had a shit day was also not a bad thing.

I didn't explain all this to the girls though; I just focussed on more simple matters.

'Look, I'm no catch, am I?' I argued, as the girls put their cups down with a synchronicity that suggested I had a double-barrelled counter argument coming my way.

'At what point do I tell somebody, *'Oh, don't worry about it or anything, but there's a distinct possibility that I might black out on our date?!''* I asked.

'Maybe it's somewhere between asking what star sign they are and asking whether they voted Leave or Remain?'

'Or should I open with, *'Just to warn you, I may fall asleep on my sofa and accidentally stand you up! Ha ha!'*

'And no thanks, I'm not about to apply to go on The Undateables, either. Much as I'd probably pass their selection criteria,' I told the girls.

Once the laughter about who they'd pair me up with on The Undateables subsided, Kay and Elle were dead set on me pursuing the most viable option and were encouraging me to go for it with PB.

'I'm just not sure there was any *spark*,' I said.

I was trying to explain why I was not as excited about this whole thing as they were. They were both sitting on the opposite side of the pub table, and being 'interviewed' like this made me feel a bit like I was on First Dates - you know that bit at the end where they show everyone banging their head on the low-hanging light before they sit down and have to awkwardly explain whether they fancy each other or not?

'From my point of view, I'd be happy to see you again - but just as friends,' one would say, usually the girl. After she'd let him pay for dinner.

'Oh yes, I was thinking the same thing!' (Yeah right).

I tried to let them down gently. 'He was nice and everything, but there was just something missing.'

'So you didn't want to jump his bones then?' said Kay, of course.

'You've hardly given it time, though,' Elle, always finding a reasonable argument, reminded me.

'You'd probably built up a picture of what you thought he'd be like, and when he didn't look exactly like you imagined, it threw you off.'

That was a good point I guess.

Elle went on, 'For example, there was nothing at all wrong with Mr Grey, Jamie Gorman is a good enough looking bloke, but when the first film came out I couldn't help being disappointed because he wasn't *my* Mr Grey. In my mind, he looked totally different.'

'You should never decide after one date unless he's a right tosser. You have to give it at least 3 dates,' Kay insisted, as if she knew much about it. She'd met her husband when she was at college and they'd been together ever since, with three lovely kids, an adorable Cockapoo and two slightly mental cats to complete the family.

'Non-dates,' I reminded them.

And so I found myself a couple of months later (Charlie's dad was really busy with his new job, and child-free weekends were few and far between) accepting a ticket to see Beyoncé at the O2.

Yep - *gulp.*

So here's the thing. Fainting isn't an Every Day issue these days. Although that's possibly because I'd gradually learned to avoid the triggers.

For example I'd given up going into any branch of a bank decades ago, and I didn't go shopping on the High Street - mostly because any type of checkout/queue situation had become my nemesis and they frown at people taking things without paying. You can imagine I am *massively* grateful for the invention of online banking and shopping - Amazon basically owns my life at this stage.

Going out to eat had sometimes been fraught too (as you've already discovered), so a couple of years ago this had been replaced by whatever was available from Just Eat. The 'green curry' chapter wasn't my only bad experience, you see...

◆

Charlie loves Wagamama, so when I needed to take him shoe shopping I promised to take him there for lunch afterwards as a ~~bribe~~ treat. I didn't shop online for his shoes, I suffered the whole 'back to school' shoe shop rigmarole and got him measured properly so that I wouldn't deform his little feet.

As with most of these non-reservation restaurants we'd had to stand in the cramped entrance area to wait for a table. We'd been standing there for about 10 minutes, quite happily chatting about the latest X-Box game, when suddenly I realised I was hitting about 4 on the Faint Scale.

I shifted my weight from foot to foot, fanned myself with the menu and followed every trick I knew to stay with it, but the damage was already done and soon after we sat down I knew I was in trouble.

I can come back from a four to five, fainting at this stage is not completely inevitable, but I had to keep nipping outside trying to *walk it off*.

I'd asked the young couple sharing our bench to keep an eye on Charlie and the three of them were looking horribly awkward about the whole thing. I could see them through the glass wall while I was pacing in circles outside, shaking my hands about trying to get my blood circulating again, clearly looking like a right nut job. But I knew I couldn't just sit back down and wait for the inevitable.

I'd told myself that once the food arrived I would feel better - perhaps I'd let myself get over-hungry so the heat from the open kitchen had got to me. But it was just taking too long! I'd kept popping outside, pacing around for a bit, then thinking I had a handle on it I'd go back in to rescue the poor couple who clearly had no experience with kids, before finding the sweats coming on again and having to get back out in the fresh air.

It was bloody *awful*, but I really didn't want to let Charlie down and I was trying to talk myself into being OK.

Being veggie I was not tempted to share Charlie's squid starter (what kind of kid was I raising to order squid!?) which had somehow arrived before our drinks - you know how random Wagamama can be. So I'd prayed for the drinks to come soon, thinking a good glug of Charlie's coke would sort me out.

In the end I'd had to give in before I created another drama.

My wonderfully understanding son went along with it without question when I asked the staff to pack our food into take away containers. Many a kid would have kicked off at their 'treat' being aborted - I was one *lucky mother* to have such a good one.

I'd felt a bit better in the fresh air and got us home safely, but I knew this had knocked my confidence about eating out too. Again, since it was just the two of us now, I didn't want to put young Charlie in the awkward position of having to sort us out if I fainted in public (or God forbid somebody made off with him when I was in no position to fight them off!), so we just stopped going.

I gave up going to the theatre too, after a different *system-failure* when my sister had treated me and Charlie to see A Christmas Carol. IBS was one of the delightful symptoms I'd had for decades, and for no particular reason I suddenly had a monstrous IBS attack.

There's no good way to say that during the first half I got *The Shits*. Big time.

Have you seen the film Bridesmaids? Even if you haven't, you probably know the scene - they go for dress fittings and suddenly they're overtaken by food poisoning. They can't hold it in and the poor Bride can't get to a loo in time so she has to squat down *letting it all go* in the middle of the road?

That's the kind of urgency we're talking about, and I had to run out to the loo every 10 minutes. I tried to hurry back because poor Charlie was sitting on his own (my sister had been on a different row with her boyfriend, having bought their tickets first), but really I'd happily have sat on the loo for the rest of the day just in case.

Obviously, EVERYBODY was tutting at me each time I got up to leave and the staff were mightily pissed off, but when you've got to go, you've got to go.

Knowing I was pissing everyone off I came over all anxious and was feeling like crap on a stick (not that what I was producing would've stuck!) so by now I was arriving at about six on my Faint Scale too.

I managed to meet up with my sister at the interval, while everyone else was collecting their pre-ordered G&T from the bar.

'God Lizzy, you look awful! Are you ok?' she asked.

Of course she took us home. I was mortified for making a fuss, for making everyone miss the rest of the production, and for stressing Charlie out again by running off all the time. So, The Theatre was added to the list of *'I can no longer get enjoyment out of...'* things.

Not that PB was to know any of this, of course, because I hadn't told him. So his idea of treating us to Beyoncé tickets was very well-meaning.

And already paid for.

Okkaayy then.

I'm not being manipulative by not telling PB... in many ways I'm probably just still in denial. In between these episodes everything is much more normal than I might've had you believe.

I have a job, albeit I've reduced my hours because I'm too knackered to cope with full-time work these days. We don't get out and about much, but Charlie loves his gaming so he's happy just having friends over to play, and I get the downtime I need to get through the weeks.

And anyway, the Doctors have always said there is nothing wrong with me, so what was there to tell?!

◆

As you know I'm fairly take-it-or-leave-it about the whole relationship thing.

Being single isn't horrible *at all*.

I like that I don't have to share the TV remote and can watch my Scandi-noir without having to compromise and watch god-awful Top Gear next time. I like that I no longer have to cook steak when I'm veggie - including Charlie's kid-friendly food I was cooking three separate meals a day and I don't miss that. I don't miss the extra laundry, ironing, or the wet towels left on the floor. I don't miss the snoring…

I mean, of course, there are *some* things I miss.

When Kay was telling us about hubby's preference for a hand-job on the sofa in front of the footy, I was both grateful I didn't have to worry about that sort of thing any more *(I still get RSI so easily!)* and a little jealous that she still had some kind of sex life to complain about.

'I guess I do sometimes miss having somebody to cuddle up with,' I was admitting to the girls.

'The trouble with dating though, especially in the early days, is that it involves more effort than being curled up in my comfy clothes on the sofa in front of Netflix, which is all I can be arsed with these days.'

We'd ordered our usual. The bloke behind the bar knew us by now and we couldn't decide if he liked our regular Friday custom, or if he whispered to the waiter, *'Oh shit, the Witches of Eastwick are here again.'*

It has to be said that sometimes we probably didn't behave very much like grown-ups. By Friday lunchtimes we were so knackered and relieved to have made it through another week that things tipped into hysteria very easily. The day Elle started a conversation by complaining about a 6 am poke in the back it all went downhill very fast.

'My house is my comfort-zone in a more pertinent way than it is for your average person. If only I could skip the stages where you have to get dressed up and *go out* on dates it wouldn't be so bad!'

'Sod that, I'd want to be wined and dined!' Kay, who knew how to get the most out of any situation, told us.

Anyway, all three of us gave me a good talking to. I could do this - I deserved a bit of fun and I hadn't fainted for ages! Nothing had really knocked my bright side nature, and I was always ready to believe I was better. I'd been looking after myself and taking the vitamins - so of course I was!

I was going to accept the invitation, and have a nice time. And that was that.

Chapter 5

All The Single Ladies

Beyoncé was shaking her famous backside about in a gold-sequined leotard. She was pretty good to be fair - I'm not exactly a fan but it's always good to broaden one's horizons. I'd been to a few concerts years ago, pre-Charlie and when my fainting was mostly under control, and I can tell you that Beyoncé was much better than a certain Jamaican-born sex symbol who'd looked thoroughly bored through her whole set. I'm not even sure she'd bothered singing as it had seemed to make no difference to what we were hearing whether she had the mic to her mouth or not. But Beyoncé was actually belting it out, so fair play.

We were in the seated area on the main floor of the arena, but of course everybody was standing up and throwing themselves about as much as possible in their half-a-square-foot of personal space.

I joined in and was happily dancing about, but being a short-arse I could hardly see a thing. I was mainly just catching glimpses of the grainy screens showing close-ups of a gloriously sweaty Queen B. I'm not ungrateful, but I did find myself thinking I could've watched this on HD TV at home and skipped the train ride, the queue to get in, the expensive snack from the food halls outside the stage area - and the heat!

Oh, God the heat! There were too many bodies...

Three. This is a tentative Three. I can come back from a Three. I'll sit down a minute. I can't really get out of here it's pretty crowded, but I'll sit down for a song or two and will feel better in a minute.

Five. I'm fanning myself now - jeez it's warm in here.

Six. Breathe normally, you'll be fine.

Eight? Ah bollocks, no it's a *niiii.....*

◆

The first thing I heard over the loud music was a woman asking, 'Would she like some chewing gum?'

What kind of shit show first-aid course had she been on!?

'Now, is everybody paying attention? This is very important! What we advise you to do in this situation is to give the semi-conscious patient a choking hazard,' *said no First Aid Trainer - ever.*

Anyway, someone rather more helpfully passed me my bottle of water and I came around enough to be taken out the back to the medical space by some burley chaps who'd appeared out of nowhere. PB wasn't allowed to come backstage with me for 'security' reasons. He hardly looked threatening, but I suppose they can't take any risks.

I had a bit more of a faint as I was being escorted around the back. The guys were very kind but for some reason they came across as slightly *amused.*

They were probably relieved not to be dealing with knife crime, which seems to be rife at the moment, and a fainting woman was probably ten-to-the-dozen at concerts.

This time I was apparently jerking about a bit. Maybe I was dancing in my 'dream', after all I could still vaguely hear the Single Ladies finale, except it sounded like it was coming from somewhere *far, far away...*

They did a quick ECG and told me there was a bit of arrhythmia, but after a bit of a lie down it had settled so they could let me go home. With the usual advice to go and see my GP in the next few days, probably just to cover their arses.

They pointed me towards the last tube before I missed it, and thank Christ I'd found PB standing awkwardly by the main doors holding my handbag and checking his watch. My phone had been in my bag so I couldn't text him to find out where he was and I'd worried he'd do a runner - without my bag with my money, tube ticket and hotel key-card I'd be right up shit creek.

The tube was packed of course, but PB bravely asked someone to give up their seat, saying *'She's just blacked out at the concert and should really sit down.'* With a tut and an eye roll one of the girls gave in and started dancing around the aisle instead - high on life and reliving the Single Ladies finale, which was handy since I'd missed it.

I was staying at a travel lodge since I was collecting Charlie from his dad's flat the next day, so I was soon in bed, feeling very embarrassed about the whole sorry affair. I sent a text to PB *'Sorry - again! Be in touch soon x'* with an embarrassed face emoji and fell into a deep sleep.

Now, what I was NOT to know, as I fell into my slumber, was that this was to be a bit of a game-changer.

I went ahead and made an appointment with my GP (I only had to wait two weeks!) to explain that I might've had some sort of mini-fit this time. And for some reason this was like activating a *secret key-word* because it triggered a whole new chain of events.

The first and most pissy thing was that I had to surrender my driving licence. This, I found out, was in case it turned out to be epilepsy. Apparently having a fit behind the wheel of a car is not a good thing.

Fuckadoodledoo, that's not particularly convenient.

The other thing it triggered was a referral to a neurologist. My GP didn't just tell me to up my antidepressants or take a few more Codeine this time! I had the golden ticket - *a referral!*

Ok, I know I sound really horrible about GPs. I don't mean to and it is not really their fault that they have to come to a conclusion about a sometimes complex situation within 10 minutes...

I saw a thing on Pinterest a little while ago which explained this quite well. I can't remember it verbatim but it was something like this:

Going to the Doctor when you are chronically ill is hard.

Imagine everything in your house is on fire, and the fire department pull up and say 'describe the fire to me and maybe we can find what caused it and put it out.'

And you have to be quick but you can't just say 'everything is on fire!', so you say 'well, the fire around the curtains is the biggest, but the fire by the photo albums is doing the worst damage. And also the sofa being on fire is really inconvenient because I could do with a sit-down.'

Occasionally the fire guy is like 'well, your TV is on fire so it could be 'electrical fireitis', but that would probably cause other things to be on fire too, like your Sky box'.

And you say 'oh yes, that's been on fire for years. I forgot to mention it because it's always been a relatively small fire compared to the sofa fire right now.'

Then you remember something else you haven't mentioned and say 'it's next to the bookcase which is quite badly on fire, too.' And the fire guy is like 'I wouldn't worry about that, bookcase fires just happen sometimes.'

◆

This may or may not make sense to you, but to me it explains the way you have to try to pick your main issue to speak to the Doctor about in your 10-minute slot. And if you do risk mentioning some other thing that's been bothering you for ages, they just dismiss it as being nothing to worry about. And they'll add things like, 'for women who've had a baby,' or 'for your age' - which annoyingly had seemed to be used as a valid reason for things at *every* age I have been so far…

And yep Doc, I'm still really tired. (I guess that's my bookcase fire.)

I have to confess my infrequent visits to my Doctor these days excluded A&E visits. By now you know I go down? And that I am generally quite clumsy...

My first breakage was at primary school when I fell down in the girls' loo. My friend went off in a panic to get the dinner lady, who didn't bother with the magic-powder placebo and instead said, 'I think it's a greenstick fracture,' which of course I'd never heard of.

Once I'd had the x-ray and was told it was indeed a greenstick fracture - which was duly plastered - I went back to school thinking the dinner lady must have super powers.

So by now I've broken my wrist twice, had two ankle avulsion fractures, a fractured vertebrae (I fell on some stairs in an old building we'd been taken to draw when I was at art college - hence my first ambulance trip) and had a few other minor accidents, sometimes through fatigue-induced numptiness. I sliced through my finger with a hedge cutter once, for example, luckily missing the tendon. A few stitches put me right.

When my wrist was still playing up two years after I broke it they gave me an MRI and decided I had *complex regional pain syndrome.* I generally make a point of trying to steer clear of anything complex so this was not the best news.

My ankle didn't heal right either and they did an MRI on that too, saying there was oedema in the joint for which they gave me an injection of cortisone, which did help for a while…

Overall, it's fair to say I'm a bit of an old banger and would be unlikely to pass an MOT.

◆

Anyway, after another disastrous non-date, what became of PB? You might think he would do a runner after twice having to witness me causing havoc by blacking out, but we did meet a few more times and I even managed to stay on my feet! But I was right - there really was no *spark*.

We'd friend-zoned each other before we even met up, I think, so the damage was already done. I also was not wholly convinced he wasn't secretly gay, but that was another matter.

We carried on with our online chat for quite a while, but he met a lovely lady on Match.com and decided to go all in with that relationship, so we drifted apart.

I was cool with that - we'd been there while we both needed somebody, and now we were both settled and OK.

I wished him luck and gave him the occasional thumbs-up on Facebook.

He sent me flowers on my birthday - for old times' sake.

Chapter 6

Everything Is Completely Normal!

Listen to this - after waiting just a few months, my neurology referral came through! They did a head MRI and guess what?

Normal!

By the way - MRIs are a piece of piss. There's a lot of hype and people get seriously scared about the idea of them, but if you ever have to have one - please don't worry! In fact I was rather relaxed - albeit it's a bit noisy - but then I'm never one to complain about a lie-down.

The normal result was obviously the *most excellent* news. I now knew with more clarity than most people that I did not have a brain tumour.

However, it was also a slightly disappointing dead-end.

I was still without my driving licence though, and the lack of a tumour or epilepsy meant I could get it back after 6 months had passed. *Hu-fuckin-rah!*

The neurologist said that although there was no epilepsy-type situation, she felt something was not quite right. In her opinion I was not just *sad*, so she referred me on again.

This time, the referral was to - hang on, this can't be right...

Geriatrics??

W.T.F? I'm only in my 30s!

It turns out that these are the guys who look into why people *fall*. Oh. Okay then.

They gave me a new set of tests, mostly of the vampire variety, but also a *tilt-table test*, which frankly I had never heard of. They didn't tell me what they were looking for and I just blindly went along with it, happy that somebody was willing to look for something at least.

So, for this test I was laid down on a special bed and strapped in with weighty Velcro at my arms, stomach and feet - it looks a bit like a Victorian torture device but it's actually pretty comfortable. They attached ECG monitors and a blood pressure cuff (do these make anyone else giggle or is it just me?) then they left me having a nice daydream for ten minutes or so.

Just when I was lovely and comfy they tilted the table up in one fairly swift move until I was almost upright. A bit like the dentist's chair but in reverse, I guess. Meanwhile, a Doctor and Nurse (I gather the tilt table was quite a new toy and they wanted to play with it, otherwise I'm sure it's usually just a nurse) had their eyes glued to a screen showing them my pulse, blood pressure and oxygen levels. They didn't talk to me; they just watched and made a few notes now and then. Which was rather unsettling.

I'll tell you now; I'd take an MRI over this *any day*.

I didn't feel well *at all*.

They aborted the test after less than 15 minutes as they said they had all the data they needed.

Thank Christ, I was just about to faint and that's not my favourite hobby. They gave me a drink of water and let me recover a bit before they sat me down for the results.

Guess what?

Not normal!

OK, wait. *Normal?*

No. *Not Normal.*

Oh.

'We think you have a type of dysautonomia known as Postural Orthostatic Tachycardia Syndrome. Most people call it POTs and we think it explains all your symptoms. Not all GPs have heard of it so it sometimes takes a few years to get a diagnosis.'

Yeah - 38, apparently.

They then asked what appeared to be an entirely random question.

'Can you bend your thumb back to touch your wrist?'

What the hell has that got to do with fainting? I wondered, showing them that I could.

'Yes, we thought you might be able to.'

Ha, if it was tricks they were after…

◆

OK, so you know on the Daily Mail website when they show a photo of a person who has an unusual diagnosis, with a ridiculously over the top 'sad-face' photo. They write the dramatic blurb about how awful the thing is and then they put the real information in a blue box at the end of the article (usually followed by a GoFundMe link)?

Well, if you can be arsed to read it, here is the blue-box information about POTs (no hard feelings if you skip it, and don't worry I don't have a GoFundMe appeal).

Postural Orthostatic Tachycardia Syndrome (POTs) can be a life-altering and debilitating chronic health condition. Simply standing up can be a challenge for people with POTs as their body is unable to adjust to gravity. POTs is characterised by orthostatic intolerance (the development of symptoms when upright that are relieved by lying down).

Symptoms include headaches, fatigue, palpitations, sweating, nausea, fainting and dizziness and are associated with an increase in heart rate from the lying to upright position of greater than 30 beats per minute, or a heart rate of greater than 120 beats per minute within 10 minutes of standing.

Postural orthostatic tachycardia syndrome is an abnormality of the functioning of the autonomic (involuntary) nervous system. To be diagnosed with POTs, an individual must experience a group of symptoms in the upright position (usually standing).

When a healthy person stands up, blood vessels contract and heart rate increases slightly to maintain blood supply to heart and brain. In POTs, this automatic adjustment to upright posture is not working correctly, resulting in an excessive rise in heart rate, increased norepinephrine in the blood and altered blood flow to the brain.

◆

OK, do you want that in English?

You've probably experienced at least one occasion where you've stood up too quickly and had a head rush, right? It lasts a fraction of a second then your body just sorts itself out.

For people with POTs, this automatic correction is fucked up. Blood pools in the lower parts of your body (hence my sexy corned beef legs) thanks to the wonders of gravity - the longer you stand still the worse it gets. Your heart rate increases to try to pull the blood back up to your brain, but your signals are all wrong, so with my type of POTs (there are different types) your blood pressure panics and drops. I don't know why, but maybe it's so you don't have a stroke or something.

From what I understand, the type of POTs where your blood pressure drops can be associated with people who have hypermobile joints, because you also have unusually elastic blood vessels which are a bit shit at keeping your blood pumping back up.

Ah… okay, the random thumb test.

Basically, the two things that should cooperate to keep you upright must've had a fall-out at work one day, because they work against each other instead.

I guess it's a bit like when the Windows 10 upgrade was forced on us all and I had to keep turning my PC off and on again to reset it. POTs is basically a bloody annoying software problem - there is usually nothing actually wrong with your heart etc. but your body needs a sort of reset...

And I now had an explanation!

Now, obviously nobody wants to be diagnosed with something that isn't easily curable. So don't go thinking I was enjoying this.

But can you imagine how it felt to finally have an explanation for this thing that had plagued me all of my life?

It was *bloody marvellous!*

And it gave me something to Google! As it did with my GP, who did exactly that at my next follow-up appointment.

As well as POTs and Joint Hypermobility Syndrome (which I didn't really see as a problem - so what if I was bendy, how could that be a bad thing?), the consultant told me that my B12 and vitamin D were still low so they prescribed a course of B12 injections.

Still?

◆

'It turns out my GP was a lying bastard!'

I was having a bit of a moan to the girls. In taking my history to get a diagnosis, the specialist had looked at my previous notes.

'You remember all those 'normal' test results? Lying git had ignored loads of things outside the normal ranges!'

It turned out that not only was my B12 and vitamin D out of range, but there were several other results which had been consistently marked by the labs as out of range - for years! OK, so they still wouldn't have jumped to a POTs-type conclusion based on any of them, but they also didn't point to just *fucking sad*.

'Lying bastard,' agreed the girls…

I have to say I took their advice and changed to a different surgery after that.

This was a big thing for me. I was the brand-loyal type, never moving banks and sticking with the same supermarket for my online groceries even when another one had some good deals that week. But I knew I wouldn't be able to trust my old GP and I didn't understand why he hadn't been more open about the test results. Maybe it was because he had me down as a depressed hypochondriac and he didn't want to give me something to actually worry about!

The consultant also mentioned in passing that I had postnatal depression on my notes - something I'd never spoken to the Doctor about at all (and never thought I had!), so I started to wonder what else was lurking in my file.

So that I could see for myself, I requested a copy of my medical notes under a Freedom of Information request. It cost me £25 and the wrath of the receptionist, but a few days later I had the full wad in my hands.

Holy hell that was happy reading.

Even I could see that the labs put the test results next to the normal range to show the Doctor how far out they are, so they'd done all the work for him...

'I'd bloody sue him!' said Kay. But heck - I was too bloody knackered to get into any of that.

Chapter 7

POTsy

'I've looked up POTs and it does make sense. I reckon my body knew it needed to not just stand still right from when I was little - all that dancing about wasn't just showing off!'

'The main thing is what now? How do they help you?' Elle asked.

She was knackered as she'd spent the morning clearing up after her lazy git of a boyfriend again, but she didn't let that stop her paying attention when it was my turn to moan. We tried to make sure we covered everyone's problems over our long Friday lunches.

'All they told me was that I have to eat lots of salt, and drink lots of water, which doesn't really make that much sense at the moment, but I'll figure it out. I'm one of the lucky ones, I don't have it nearly as bad as some people!' I told them.

I'd done a bit of Googling of course, so I knew there were people out there with POTs who couldn't stand up even for a minute and had to use a wheelchair to get about - and even worse there were some who were bedbound.

Most days, as long as I moved around (which I now realise increases circulation, making sure blood gets up to your brain) I could manage.

Sometimes on a really hot day, especially if it was a bit humid too like the 'green curry' day, I did feel rough even without standing up to aggravate the problem. But I was coping pretty well in comparison.

It's a good job I wasn't harbouring any talents though - it'd be a terrible waste if I'd been born with the voice of an angel because I'd never be able to get up on stage to perform.

And it's lucky I chose a sit-down career - my dad had been quite determined that I should become a hairdresser and all that standing up would've been no good.

> *Mum and dad hadn't understood my desire to go to art college, and seeing no future in it dad had tried to come up with alternative careers. In those days young ladies were most often directed towards secretarial college, but I'd been doing a weekly blue rinse for my elderly neighbour for years by now, and I'd regularly cut mum and dad's hair, and permed my sister's (it was acceptable in the 80s), so dad said I had a natural talent and would never be out of work if I got myself trained. But it just wasn't what I had in mind and with dad gone by then, mum gave in about the art college thing, since I'd got a grant, and passed the entrance interview...*

The consultant came up with a theory about why it'd all kicked off again in my 30s. She'd noted that soon after Charlie started nursery he'd brought home every bug going, as a lot of kids do. He was a tough cookie and shook them off normally, but since I was feeble I'd picked them up from him and not shaken them off.

I'd got Strep Throat 11 times in one year - one time it had turned into Scarlet Fever. *(I thought that had died out in Shakespearean times!)*.

I'd been pretty bloody poorly for a year or so and had hardly been off antibiotics, so in the end they decided I needed my tonsils out.

Jesus on a pogo stick, what a bloody nightmare that was!

The pre-op check had picked up some arrhythmia so the anaesthetist had come and had a word, reassuring me that he would keep an eye on things.

Um, thanks.

After the op I'd had to stay in overnight for observation and I have to say it was hardly Hotel Paradise, thanks mostly to a very mentally unstable old lady on the ward who'd kept stripping down to naked and shrieking like a Banshee. The poor woman was clearly very confused and the staff had real problems calming her down and protecting her modesty (and our eyes). I mean, it was nobody's fault, but when you've just had an op you really want a peaceful night to get over it. Instead it was all rather stressful and upsetting.

The following morning they made no secret of the fact that they needed my bed back ASAP. I was throwing up like a good'un - anaesthetics clearly didn't agree with me - and every time I'd got up to get dressed I'd had to lie back down again. I was just catching myself before I hit the deck. I have to say the staff, whose nerves had been frazzled by the old lady for the last 8 hours, had no sympathy and kept hurrying me up.

After all it was only a tonsillectomy…

They finally sent me on my way with my sister, who'd arrived to drive me home, with a sick bowl and some painkillers. But I'd had to keep stopping in the corridor to throw up and sit down so I didn't pass out.

I'll tell you now - puking your guts up when your throat is raw having had your diseased tonsils burned off is horrendous.

I'd kept trying to make progress so I could just get home to lie down, but I was really having trouble staying upright long enough to get anywhere. The bright corridors with their coloured stripes leading to the way out had seemed endless.

A nice nurse who happened to be passing nipped off for a clean sick bowl - since mine was pretty full by now - commenting to my sister that she couldn't believe they'd sent me away in such a state. We were rule followers though, and wouldn't have thought to stand our ground and refuse to leave, so off we went again.

We finally made it to the car and after we'd set off I fainted in the passenger seat - my poor sister was trying to concentrate on driving while checking I was still breathing and not choking on my own vomit. I was out for the count and she was just about to turn back and head to A&E when I finally woke up.

'I'll be OK, please just get me home,' I'd pleaded pitifully.

It took a while to shake this whole episode off, but the good news was that once I'd healed from the op I finally stopped getting Strep Throat.

The problem was I'd started to really need an afternoon nap, and the consultant said it was probably Post Viral Fatigue, since the infection had got such a tight hold of me for a while there.

The consultant explained that POTs can get worse after certain events, such as: pregnancy and childbirth *(tick)*, infection/illness *(tick)*, operations/anaesthetics *(tick)*, B12 deficiency *(tick)*, injury *(tick)*, and periods of stress, such as divorce *(tick, tick...)*.

Boom!

Chapter 8

Number One Person

A few years have passed since I got my POTs diagnosis, and nothing much has changed. I eat the salt and I drink the water.

Charlie has moved up to Big School and he's still a superstar. He's clever, funny, kind... his class gave out spoof certificates at the end of the first year and Charlie's said '*Most Thoughtful Person.*' I am immensely proud of the young man he's becoming, and while some parents despair at their teens turning a bit Emo - I of course think it's fabulous!

Like me he's pretty shy, but he has a few really lovely close friends. Having inherited my red-brown hair (not that anybody would know since I've been Nice 'n Easy *Light Ash Blonde* for about twenty years), he's overtaken me in height.

He doesn't just have my blue eyes though - his dad's dark brown colouring must've also influenced the outcome and he has the most amazing *kaleidoscope* eyes. He's now lanky and awkward but starting to know himself. You know that stage when music is suddenly everything?

He's so far managed to avoid the school bullies by being the 'grey-man', quietly going about his business and not attracting too much attention. Being a *top set* lad he didn't cross paths with them too often.

I've always tried to do fun things with him in the school holidays, like going out and collecting tadpoles and making them a home in a tank, with rocks and appropriate plants, until they grew all their legs and we released the little frogs back into the pond. But as my health dipped I couldn't keep it up for the whole holidays, so he'd needed to be tooled up with tech to keep him occupied.

Which he wasn't likely to complain about because it was every boy's dream.

Over the years he's collected a Wii, Wii U, Xbox, PlayStation, DS, PS3 and his latest favourite - an iPad mini. His dad paid half for most of these things for birthdays and Christmases over the years. It sounds like he's properly spoiled but he never asked for big things - we decided to get them for him because his Christmas lists always consisted of much more modest requests like the latest Skylander (about £10) which of course he was treated to as well.

Having allowed him to move his gaming gear out of the lounge and into his bedroom when he reached the ripe age of 13 (we had the online *stranger-danger* talk first) he's now one of those teens who lives in his bedroom, permanently attached to technology.

OF COURSE, I've always felt like the worst parent ever, and I habitually avert my eyes when the Sky News app on my phone publishes articles about too much screen time being bad for kids.

But I *am* keeping him alive so it could be worse.

He's always been pretty accepting of our version of 'normal', but there was one occasion a few years ago when I was lying on the sofa feeling like a sack of shit tied in the middle. The poor lad crept up and leaned right into my face before gently poking me.

'I was just checking you weren't dead' he'd said, pretty matter of factly, before going back to watching Good Mythical Morning on YouTube.

(Rhett and Link had been in hysterics after eating a variety of strange things. Apparently this is how to get rich in today's world).

We're doing ok, anyway - we've got a decent routine going. I honestly *love* my little job. I'm a part-time communications officer at a school (yes, they have those these days!) and I was very, very lucky that the job came along when I needed it. Not only do the hours suit me, but in the past I'd had jobs that scared the shit out of me - sure they'd find me out for blagging sooner or later. I mean that never actually happened, but I was always lacking in confidence. I'd won awards for previous campaigns, been promoted, and had always been praised for my attitude (remember I'm *nice*, and I wasn't a jobs-worth) but I could never quite believe I was a grown up doing actual proper work.

I knew I couldn't cope with that kind of stress these days though, so now I basically just hang out on Facebook posting nice news, like the kids raising money for a clean-water tap to be installed in India (they raised over £1,000!), and who can't do that?

I built the school a new website too, which saved them a bunch of money as they thought they'd have to get someone in to do that, but my old graphic design background and knack for picking up new technology came in handy.

After school I usually go back to bed for a while. Charlie is always keen to get into his room to start gaming anyway, and I get up in time to feed him and help with his homework.

I only work three days a week, so on the other two days I drop Charlie off to his school in the morning, then I usually go back to bed to get some extra rest. This way I can be up for more of the weekend while Charlie is around. It works to a degree.

Pacing, they call it.

I've hired a dog walker now, and our poor fat dog has lost lots of weight, so she's happier. She'd got obese when my symptoms had flared up and I didn't have the energy to walk her every day. The dog walker has a key to the house so if I'm in bed she lets herself in to collect Lillie - who after her walk runs back upstairs to find me and throws herself on my bed with her tail wagging, as if she's saying *'Guess where I've been! I went to the beach! It was great!!'*

By now I've passed the Big *Four Ohhh!* We had a BBQ on the pebble beach with the family which was nice and relaxed.

I'm not saying I ever feel *well,* and while I do my best for Charlie I'm not exactly mum of the year, but he certainly isn't my carer or anything as bad as that.

I don't expect him to do jobs around the house - as long as he does his homework I'm happy to let him be a kid for as long as possible. The world will soon start pissing on his head, after all...

People might think I'm a bit soft because I don't make Charlie help with the cleaning (I certainly had to at his age), but I suppose because I'd failed at keeping our family together, I feel I owe him.

I'd been certain that me and his dad would stick together, and after we'd been together for 20 years I was gutted to become another divorce statistic. So Charlie not having a dad in the house makes me feel incredibly guilty. It all happened when he was really young so he knows no different, but I do, and I can't help feeling bad about it.

Now then, let's be honest. There was obviously more to us splitting up than just drifting apart. I don't want you thinking we didn't try for Charlie's sake, because we did. But I would never bad-mouth Charlie's dad and I don't think he would do that to me either, so we'll keep our problems to ourselves. I hope you don't mind...

'Charlie is growing up fast and doesn't need you so much these days Lizzy,' Kay had recently said, while spitting out the churros she'd just bitten into from our sharing platter full of goodies. *'Urgh that's disgusting!* What happens when he leaves home and you're left on your own?'

OK, so I won't lie. It's been a few years since the PB non-dates and the truth is - I am starting to *look*. I don't mean I've started to prowl the aisles of my local Tesco's for a new man, but I guess I've started noticing nice looking blokes again.

You know, taking a second-glance and smoothing down my hair when a particularly good looking delivery guy knocks on the door, that kind of thing.

I was starting to feel a little bit conflicted about my resolution to remain single, but I would never want Charlie to think he was not my Number One Person...not after all he's had to put up with.

Kay was right though, Charlie was hanging out with his friends more. He was often out at weekends while I was home alone (waiting for the teen-Uber text, when I'd head out and gather up the crew and drop them all to their respective homes. *Does that make me too nice?*) and maybe I was starting to get a little bit - oh god...

Lonely!

Chapter 9

Bye-Bye, D

Wait, wait... I can't do this.

I have to be honest with you.

I've already told you some pretty embarrassing shit, but I'm even more embarrassed talking about this than I was telling you about actually getting The Shits at the theatre (which was not a one-off, you understand).

I tried, you see - I sort of met somebody... A friend of a friend told me about this chap who'd got divorced and she decided to introduce us. 'He's a real family man,' she'd said...

I was going to skip the whole sorry tale, mainly because I didn't want to give him ANY kind of recognition whatsoever. Because in fact he turned out to be a disgusting excuse for a human being. And you know that song 'you're so vain, you probably think this song is about you.' Well, I kind of didn't want to acknowledge him in any way which might make him feel he'd mattered, you know? But it wouldn't be fair on you guys to pretend I hadn't tried, so here goes.

I'm not going to use his name, though - I can't bring myself to. It gets stuck in my throat. He'd become known as Dickhead among enlightened circles, so that's what he'll be known as, ok?

Dickhead was a salesman. And believe me he knew how to sell himself. He wasn't nice looking - he looked more like Shrek's white cousin. He was of a rather large build (less *nice* people might say he was fat), had kind of a big head and a thick head of unruly blonde hair. I didn't really care about any of this at the time though.

Charlie's dad had been *handsome*. I'd always thought he was out of my league and he turned heads when we went out. Not that he'd have noticed because he was a good man and didn't have a wandering eye, but we'd be standing at a bar and people would stop us and make a comment. In our younger days he'd get really embarrassed when people said he looked like Tom Cruise, and I'd often felt people were thinking *what's he doing with her?* but friends told me I was being a numpty and that we were well suited. Not that I'd ever thought looks were important, but I was a bit longer in the tooth now so I was very aware that they were not *at all.*

I'd *thought* Dickhead was a nice, jolly man with a lust for life, and in a funny way it was nice not to feel like I was with somebody who was *out of my league.*

He'd appeared to treat me well, and in the early days he did seem caring, thoughtful and good fun. We only saw each other now and then to start with, so I guess it was easy enough for him to be attentive in such short bursts.

But what he actually turned out to be was a Class A Narcissist.

Kay and Elle's other halves hadn't liked him. We'd had get-togethers from time to time, usually a BBQ in Kay's back garden so we didn't have far to take her for a lie down when she got pissed on two sips of prosecco, and the lads had gathered around the fire (as they do) with their beers.

The girls had reported back afterwards that their fellas didn't think Dickhead was good enough for me, and that really I could do so much better. I hadn't really paid that much attention, thinking they were just being a bit over-protective.

It turned out that my family had felt the same way, but they hadn't shared their opinion at the time. They said it was up to me who I spent my time with and would never dream of interfering. I respected that, and I think I needed to figure it out for myself in order to really believe it, anyway. Proven by the fact that the girls trying to warn me off had gone over my head.

I was always an *all in* person - I love big, and since I don't like failure I can be slow to realise that things are not working out too well. However, over time Dickhead had become more... *evasive*. He'd had more work functions, which of course I was not invited to, and he'd had to go abroad for *meetings*. To Vegas, for example.

He'd been generous at times, giving me presents like an iPad for Christmas and a Kindle for my Birthday, which were things I couldn't have bought myself on my part-time pay. OK, he'd got them for free from work, but they still had a value to me!

Not that I was materialistic, but the presents had seemed well-chosen, to give me things to occupy me when I was tired and crashed out on the sofa (in between being his slave - he never lifted a finger, but I guess he did work more hours…).

He'd told me I was beautiful and had said he was really lucky to have a second chance at love, especially with somebody so nice.

I'm really ashamed that I couldn't see what was rotten behind his words - *and, oh god, I'd introduced him to Charlie!*

He was on good money from his medical-supplies sales job and he'd seemed….. *respectable.* But as any salesman worth his salt would do, he did just what he needed to close the sale. He was nice for just long enough. Then there was a period of denial, until eventually I started to see the cracks.

It was little things at first - I noticed he was locking himself away in the loo for far longer than was necessary, *at least for somebody who didn't have IBS.* And he'd always take his phone with him. His phone was always locked, and he'd turn the screen away when he read messages, which would always be 'just work'.

I also started to notice that the jolly side was in fact a bit mean. His jokes were usually at somebody else's expense and he made nasty comments about how people looked, including teasing Charlie about his red hair.

How very 1980s of him. These days - thanks in no small way to Prince Harry and Ed Sheeran - having red hair really isn't something a kid should be teased about.

But he was no looker himself, so 'Pot, meet Kettle,' came to mind.

We met a plain-looking lady and her kids when we were out one day and he'd looked really panicked. I'd asked him why he looked so flustered and he said it was because she was a client and he couldn't remember her name, so he didn't want to seem rude when it came to introductions.

I later found out they'd gone away for a dirty little weekend. He'd told me that trip was a work-incentive with a male colleague. He might really have forgotten her name for all I know, but he'd certainly known her pretty intimately for a couple of days - *dirty sod.*

He'd begun to start arguments too. He seemed to thrive on drama, or maybe it was just a distraction technique. I'm not one for arguing, but he'd lie about really obvious things and when I queried what he was saying, because I'd genuinely get confused by the changing details, he'd try to tell me I was imagining things. If I queried lipstick on his collar, or glitter on his dinner jacket he'd always have some excuse.

'One of my team was cold in her strappy dress so I let her borrow my jacket for a while. It must have brushed off her,' and such like.

He'd always say that I was paranoid, and he'd laugh at me for being stupid. Until one day I found out what he was really up to.

I'd kept hearing a *beep! beep!* after he'd gone out to another work do, and I eventually followed the sound to a drawer where I discovered he had several mobile phones tucked away.

Okkaaayyy then.

He'd forgotten to silence one phone and from the notifications on the screen it was clear he had some extracurricular activity going down.

He'd told me he wasn't on any dating sites or apps, and that he really liked me - that he wanted to give us a chance to see where things went.

But this *beeping* phone told me he had several dating profiles, and he was exchanging messages and meeting up with at least seven different women. In fact the messages were quite gag-making, and I'm not that much of a prude.

That night he'd planned to stay over after his work do. He'd usually crawl in at about 3am and crash out next to me, snoring like a walrus. I'd woken up at about 4am and found the room quiet, so I wasn't sure if he'd made it back safely - he wasn't averse to getting so pissed he'd lose his phone and wallet and end up wandering the streets with his bow tie hanging out of his top pocket. So I went downstairs to see if he'd fallen asleep on the sofa, or if he'd perhaps worked out that I must've found his secret phone stash and legged it.

Oh, do I wish!

I opened the lounge door and walked in on him with the laptop perched on the oak coffee table, his trousers and boxers around his ankles, sex-skyping some woman - in my lounge! He'd put his headphones on so that I wouldn't hear the girl talking to him, but of course then he didn't hear me coming in, either.

Good God, it was a sight I'll never un-see.

With his bulging eyes rolling back and his tongue half out of his dribbling mouth, he looked disgusting and ridiculous in equal measures, especially when he noticed me standing in the doorway and fumbled around unsure whether to cover himself up first or to slam the laptop shut!

Having had a night on the Jagerbombs his reflexes were clearly a bit slow so this all unfolded in a strange Matrix-like slow motion.

Now, I know some women would be heartbroken, or hysterically angry about this scene. But mostly I just wanted to laugh! The only thing that pissed me off was that he was having a bare-arsed tug on my nearly-new sofa.

He could've put a bloody towel down!

But there is a certain calmness that comes from knowing you're not going mad after all.

Charlie was with his dad that weekend and by the time he got home Dickhead was long gone. There was a bit more to the whole sorry tale - he tried to do me out of quite a bit of money as a parting gesture, and I found out he'd been sexually harassing a girl at work (until her Polish builder boyfriend offered to ask him to leave her alone), but we live and learn.

I had a few offers from protective male friends who said they'd make sure he left me *well* alone, if you know what I mean, but I was too nice to consider that type of action and luckily he went on his way - no doubt onto his next victim.

It transpired that I'd been his 'cover'. *I know there's another term for this but I can't bring myself to use it - if you know what I mean you can keep that to yourself.* I'd been the respectable one he could take along to meet the family and attend the occasional formal work do, where he knew I wouldn't show him up to clients. But what he really wanted was to hit strip shows in Vegas, and take women back to his hotel room when he was away with work, and pick up strangers to go dogging...

Gross.

I blocked his number from my phone, blocked him on Facebook and left the whole sorry episode behind me. It was actually really easy to move on - the moment I worked out what a Dickhead he was I was over it. He emailed me about a year later saying he was *sorry*, and that I'd *deserved better*, but I didn't give him the satisfaction of a reply. When I realised it was just more self-indulgent bullshit I hit delete, then went straight to my trash folder and deleted it from there too so I couldn't be tempted to get drawn in.

Do you want to hear something truly amazing? The girl he'd been having webcam sex with - at the same time as seeing me and picking up all these other women to shag in car parks, and who had seen me come into the room while they were *at it* moved in with him a few months later!

And get this - I've recently heard that they are getting married! Not only is it amazing that she was actually real and he wasn't just being cat fished *(don't say shame!)* but what sort of grown-up relationship starts like that?

Is that how it is these days?

In that case you can count me right out!

So yes, much as I would happily pretend none of that had ever happened, I had tried dating and I'd got my fingers burned. I mean, who can be arsed with this shit?

So what now? I didn't want to expose me and Charlie to another terrible mistake, and it seemed like I couldn't trust my own judgement, so was I destined to be alone for the rest of my life?

Where even is the Cats Protection League?

Chapter 10

The Hip Bone's Connected To The...

On a routine visit to my new Doctor (when you have B12 injections they have to check your blood now and then to see if you still need it), I dared to ask a 'small fire' question.

I wanted to understand if it was normal to be in *this much* pain, and to be *this tired* with POTs. I mean, I get the fainting thing now, but I've never understood why I hurt everywhere and wanted to sleep all day. He'd referred me to physio a couple of years ago for a particularly evil bout of sciatica and I'd really benefited from a short course of treatment - after a typical NHS three month wait, the chap I finally saw had been bloody marvellous.

Chris was lovely - chilled out, tall, athletic and ever-so-slightly hipster, with magic hands.

What I liked best was that he allowed me to keep my sense of humour. I know their time is precious, but when it's all business it's a bit morbid, so my ability to laugh at life helps a lot. He told me that I'd developed a bit of scoliosis and over a few sessions he helped to straighten me out a bit.

This was obviously great, but I was actually hurting pretty much everywhere and that referral had only been for my back problem (that had been an *inferno* on the day I saw my GP) so it was all he could help me with.

I'd joined a Facebook group for people with POTs, and although some of the other members talked about tiredness and a few talked about pain, POTs didn't seem to be the only explanation for how I was feeling.

Some people were really active and went to the gym, or went running (something I could not do in my wildest dreams these days), but once they had their fainting under control they didn't have other issues to contend with. On the other hand I was also reminded that others were so bad they were wheelchair-bound, so I wondered if I was just kind of in the middle.

Mrs Average, that's me.

Having picked up from the POTs consultant that my inflammation markers had been elevated (and ignored) for several years, he referred me to Rheumatology.

'Perhaps it's a touch or arthritis,' he said

My appointment came through but it was for quite a few months later, so mum took pity and paid for me to see a private specialist.

He decided that I had *Fibromyalgia* as well as POTs.

I didn't exactly relish this new diagnosis for the following reasons: 1) almost everybody thinks fibromyalgia is kinda made up (like they did with yuppie flu) so it wasn't going to help me to be understood (I could almost hear my mum saying *'oh that'll be your bruised bones then'*), and 2) there is not much they can do about it.

I was prescribed Gabapentin, though.

Oh, this would be the answer to everything, right?

It was a *proper drug* after all?

OK, for those who don't know, Gabapentin is an anticonvulsant drug which they use *off-label* to treat chronic pain conditions. I guess it turns off something in the brain; I'm not sure how it works.

It somehow turned off some of the pain, *yes - result!* And I was sleeping much better. After years of insomnia I'd said if only I could get 4 hours sleep a night I would never *ever* complain again, and here I was getting at least 6 hours!

It also pretty much got rid of my Restless Legs Syndrome so I didn't end up doing the River Dance for half the night *(a rather fun-sounding affliction that was anything but, but you'll only know if you've had it)* so it was all sounding pretty fabulous, right?

The problem is that every silver lining has a cloud, and it had side-effects. It left me feeling really sedated - despite the extra sleep - and I'd started to have trouble finding my words. Either I couldn't think of a word at all - by which I mean it could be something really simple, like 'coffee,' and I'd stand there floundering, clicking my fingers in the air waiting for the word to come. Or my words would get muddled like they'd been mixed up in a giant cocktail shaker. Charlie's favourite was when I said we needed to find a space in the *par cark...*

Of course the two of us laughed about it, it was just so silly. Charlie would look up from under his floppy fringe with a wry smirk and wait for the penny to drop, and then we'd have a good giggle.

One time we were driving up the road and a little Jack Russell ran out of somebody's driveway. It looked like he was about to run into the road and I called out *'arrgghhh horse!'* as I started to brake.

I'm sure I will never live that one down!

I was putting together a new Ikea desk for Charlie's bedroom one day and we were discussing the best place for it. When I said, *'Maybe we can move the trampoline somewhere else,'* he just grinned at me. He's too young to dare to say *'What the fuck?'* out loud, but I know he was thinking it. I'd meant his keyboard (of the musical variety).

As a communications officer it was rather vital that I could *do words* so this was all shits and giggles, but work-wise it was a bit of a problem. I tried to take the rough with the smooth and carried on taking it - after all some people swore by it.

Meanwhile not only did my brain forget how to *do words*, it forgot how to move me about safely too. As somebody who had on previous occasions been a little clumsy (ahem) even I noticed this was much worse since I'd started to take the pills. I'd go to walk out of a room, miss the gap and ricochet off the door frame, leaving me with an achy arm for days.

My hands forgot how to work properly too and I'd just let go of things - like a full glass of ~~wine~~ (cough) water! People would look at me like I was a right mental case because it totally looked like I did it on purpose!

I was told it was the best option, though and so I carried on with no discernible change for a couple more years, during which time I found safety on my sofa and solace in Netflix, and in reading soppy books on my Kindle.

Charlie was doing his own thing most of the time these days, either in or out of the house. I was finding myself without the energy to do the kinds of things I might've done had things turned out differently (I'd always pictured us packing up picnics, kites and the dog and heading to Dartmoor like I did as a kid) but at the same time I was sometimes a bit *bored!*

I was at peace with my declining health and my advancing years but I still had head space to fill. So I started to live vicariously through the characters in my books, or on the TV - which I know sounds *really fucking sad*. But so what if I didn't have much of a life? I could daydream up a fantasy one instead!

I started to work my way through book after book on the Kindle's *recommended for you* list. As a Prime member, since you might recall shopping was not my thing, I got the odd book for free so I ended up reading things I probably wouldn't have picked off a shelf. A series by Nicole Snow made *50 Shades* look like nursery rhymes, which was rather unexpected and made me come over all unnecessary...

Back in the day I used to enjoy a biography, or a crime drama, but these days rom-coms mostly hit the spot.

They don't need a massive attention span to work out whodunit clues, I don't need to be fully engaged with complex characters - I can put a rom-com down and not be left with the suspense of what happens next because after the first chapters you kinda knew which characters would get off with each other. They were reassuringly predictable, and I could swoon over the lead male - all rugged and sexy - without having to put any makeup on.

Just what the Doctor ordered.

I was also partial to a box-set but I had limited self-control and would find myself binge-watching, staying up past my bedtime for just one more episode.

Netflix would pop a message up on screen, *'Just checking you're still watching,'* which reminded me of Charlie's *'Just checking you're not dead'* enquiry some years ago.

At least they cared.

The problem is that these rom-coms started to put me *in the mood* for romance, and I found myself daydreaming away the days. One character in my fantasies was built around a poor unsuspecting chap who spends a lot of time at his allotment...

Ok, I know that sounds really, really square but let me explain. *(Ha ha I can't remember the last time I used the word square like that - possibly in the 80s!).*

When they built our little housing development they put in a small allotment site on the opposite side of the road.

With an open view across the allotment gardens to the rolling East Devon countryside, I've always thought this was rather nice and certainly better than being overlooked by another row of bedroom windows.

There are a few regulars - mostly retired gentlemen who arrive at the same time every day, have a bit of a poke around with a garden fork, water their sprouts, then unfold a deckchair for a rest.

However, there's this one chap who can't be much older than me - it's hard to tell because his plot is further back from the road and not quite close enough to see - who spends all day Saturday and all day Sunday on his plot.

All weekend, every weekend. And some evenings, too.

He chats to his neighbours, works in his greenhouse, cuts the grass in between everybody's plots *(how nice)* and before long I'd created a whole back-story about this chap. I wasn't purposely staring at him or anything, but my bedroom is at the front of the house and I'd stand at the window on Sundays doing the ironing...

◆

Now, ironing can be a bit challenging for people with POTs. By setting up by the window the breeze helps to keep me cool, and when I stand there to use the ironing board my bed is right behind me. This is handy for regularly flopping down to abort the pre-syncope that would come on after ironing a couple of Charlie's school shirts.

The whole *getting the ironing done* thing can take some time, taking into account the rests (although I admit some of them were purely procrastination, favouring a few levels of Candy Crush over doing more ironing), and all this time allotment man is just *there.*

The kitchen window also faces that way, so every time I make a coffee, or a sandwich, or Charlie's tea... you get the idea. If he doesn't turn up one day I get quite worried about him. I have no idea where he actually lives. He arrives by car so he wasn't from our housing development. But clearly he's single, *right?* I mean he wouldn't spend that much time over there on his own if he had a nice wife and kids at home would he?

When the weather was freezing, or if it was particularly rainy, I wondered if I should take him over a cup of tea.

When the weather was hot I wondered if I should take him a glass of cold lemonade...

Maybe we'd get into a conversation, and perhaps one day he'd offer to show me his prize-winning marrow!?

I wondered if I should just pop over and say hello, but of course I never did. I confess that, without thinking of it as stalking in any way (after all it wasn't my fault I could see him while I went about my business in my own house, was it?) this went on for quite a while. I wasn't obsessed or anything, and he didn't cross my mind in between times, but I suppose that when I looked up from the ironing board and noticed him there it was a nice distraction.

Maybe one day we'd bump into each other and a romance would, ahem... grow?

Well, that was until one Sunday afternoon. I was several shirts into the ironing when I noticed all the allotment holders had gathered in their gated car park.

What in heaven's name...?

Has allotment-man got a plant pot *on his head?*

Oh, so has that one (never seen him before, his plot must be down the bottom corner). And now they're all putting plant pots on their heads.

What the fuck is this?

They then paraded out of the car park, each pushing a wheelbarrow, and in single file they walked up to the top of the road. The road comes to a dead end and they gathered there looking like a weird collection of overgrown gnomes.

The next thing I knew a bearded fella was blowing a whistle, some music started playing, and they all began sort-of *Morris Dancing* down the road with their wheelbarrows and plant-pot-hats.

Can you imagine?

Is this a Devon thing? I know we're an odd bunch sometimes - indeed only yesterday somebody posted on the local Facebook community page, *'Anybody lost a pig?'* with a photo of a fat pig posing on their front lawn like it's a totally normal occurrence. *'She's mine, I'm on my way to collect her!'* was posted underneath, although I'm not sure how they'd prove it. She might be bacon for all we know.

But even I've never seen this behaviour before.

Of course I stood at the window and watched them practice this odd routine, rather like an extremely low-budget Red Arrows, as they criss-crossed and skipped down the road occasionally losing an ill-fitting plant pot hat along the way. Whistle man was clearly head gnome, and they seemed to have a bit of a routine down after a while.

What this meant was that I got a closer look at allotment man, since he was now passing right by my front door, and I won't lie - I totally went off him!

Maybe it was the fact that having seen him properly, he was no longer a 'fictional' character - he wasn't just a hazy, distant personification of someone who mainly existed in my imagination.

Allotment man was *real*.

And he *skipped*.

Not that he'd have been bothered that I'd gone off him; he didn't even know I existed after all. It's not like I'd seen him gazing longingly up at my steam-sweaty face at the bedroom window.

I later found out that they were rehearsing for the town carnival, and with some perspective it seemed a little less ludicrous, but all the same.

So I moved on, and over time I found out that *fantasy me* didn't have A Type. Of course in my own daydreams I wasn't always knackered, accident-prone, and fainty. No, I was fit and energetic and fun!

I was the *me* I might've been, if only...

So one day *fantasy me* might have the hots for Jason Momoa - all strong, tall, bearded and tattooed - you know, all manly. (Except I read that in real life he's also a thinking man and that was very attractive. He's studied marine biology, and he spent time painting in Paris!).

Not that I'd online stalked him of course, but the man was totally swoon-worthy.

However the next day, fantasy me was admiring the *can't-put-my-finger-on-it* quality of Jonny Lee Miller in Elementary, or a devoted Ryan Gosling as seen in The Notebook... Don't worry, I shall always remain loyal to my first crush David Bowie, but it's hard to fantasise about somebody who is no longer alive.

You'd think this lack of *type* would make things easier and maybe open up the field a bit. But in real life of course my *field* was really very small, since I never really went out any more.

And I flatly refused to go online shopping for a man...

OK, truth be known it wasn't so much the *shopping* that was the real problem - it was almost certainly the being *shopped for* that I couldn't contemplate. I may have finally accepted that I had a redeeming quality – I'm *nice*, but nobody chooses something *nice*. That's way too mediocre. I mean, you don't order something from Amazon with a 2-3 star rating - you change the search criteria to 4 stars and above as a minimum, right? And realistically, I wasn't a four-star prospect. It didn't matter really, because I didn't have the energy for real-life romance anyway, did I?

I really didn't need a man to get by. I'd never had *pink* and *blue* jobs, and I was perfectly capable of *being* single. When the oven broke I replaced the thermostat. When the car broke down I had an intelligent chat about what needed doing with the mechanic and found a way to half the repair cost. I put up my own shelves and painted my own walls...

Sometimes I have to wear a back brace or wrist support to tackle jobs, but I've always been the more practical one in my family (as I was in my marriage), and I usually find a way to do whatever needs doing. You can find instructions for just about everything on YouTube these days, so there's no excuse not to, really.

Not *needing* somebody around made me much less desperate than other people I knew, who'd hit up Match.com the moment they found themselves single. One friend was making a good job of renovating her house by going through tradesmen - the latest fella had done a lovely job of decorating her entrance area.

But I was much more self-sufficient and was in no hurry to alter the situation really.

So, I would just keep lighting the candles and having romantic evenings in on my own - letting my mind go to places my body wasn't willing to...

Chapter 11

Personal Independence

I was pretty good at putting my health problems to the back of my mind and just getting on with things. I didn't like to dwell on what wasn't going to kill me, after all. But I'd taken stock of my new reality recently and opened my eyes to that fact that here I was: a single mum, only well enough to work 18 hours a week, 39 weeks a year, at a low-grade school admin job. My ambitious years were a dim memory.

Money was tight, but it wasn't exactly my fault I was not working full-time. I'd planned to - by now with Charlie being settled at big school there was no reason not to work more hours - other than the fact that I was not well enough. I'd always been a grafter, but since my shitty health was holding me back, I wondered…

…was it bad enough to qualify me for some help?

I was in a bit of debt, no thanks to having to change my car for a more sensible one. My old BMW was a bit heavy for my painful shoulder these days - if I wasn't careful it would dislocate, and the low seat position gave my back a hard time. So I ignored the nagging bank balance and traded it in for a used Fiesta with a smaller engine and nice light steering.

I'd also gone over my grocery budget too often, relying on expensive home-delivery pizza during a particularly knackered phase.

And when we'd bought the house I hadn't budgeted for a dog walker or expensive prescription dog food, either.

All in all, a few extra pennies would certainly help and I'd seen on the Facebook page that lots of POTs patients had been successful in claiming Personal Independence Payments (PIP). Some worked, some couldn't.

I hated the idea really, but being strapped for cash made me look into it, and I found that in order to claim, you must be aged 16 to 64 and have a health condition or disability where you:

- have had difficulties with daily living or getting around (or both) for 3 months

- expect these difficulties to continue for at least 9 months (unless you're terminally ill with less than 6 months to live)

Hmm, sounds not unlike me, do you think?

I did a bit of soul-searching and decided that it would be reasonable to apply.

The form arrived in the post and Jesus Christ it took me a bloody *age* to fill it in. You have to return it within a set deadline so you can't take too much time over it. There's no online version either, so you can't type it out and save it, and I find holding a pen actually quite sore (the chap that diagnosed fibro told me I have osteoarthritis in my hands) so I could only write a bit at a time before it became illegible.

I had to do it in *sittings.*

The other problem was that my Gabapentin brain had a very poor recollection of events and I had to keep thinking back to which Doctor I had seen and when - going over the last decade in more detail than I could even remember yesterday. That copy of my medical notes I'd got hold of turned out to be really helpful.

The PIPsters aren't interested in what conditions you *have* - you can tell them you've been diagnosed with 100 different conditions and they don't care. What they want to know is how it *affects* you. So I had to describe, in many places on the same form, the fact that I get tired, am in pain, I black out... *blah blah blah.*

Then despite an *incredible* level of detail being requested in the forms, and the fact that the application was supported with letters from specialists and consultants, I was then called in for a face-to-face assessment. Standard.

This was one of the most joyous occasions in my life.

You are advised that, 'You'll be asked questions about your ability to carry out activities and how your condition affects your daily life. The meeting will take about an hour.'

Pissing perfect.

◆

Now, let's talk about mornings. Almost nobody likes mornings, right?

I know. They're shit.

If you do, frankly you're weird.

Now imagine your body doesn't cope with the transition from lying down, to upright. Take that situation and multiply it *a lot of times* due to the fact that you've been lying down all night - and you can imagine that jumping out of bed full of the joys of spring just doesn't happen.

But there's more - a body with widespread chronic pain seizes up overnight, so just rolling out of bed feels nearly impossible. I grab the sheets to try to pull myself over to one side so I can work from there, but then my hands hurt or a shoulder pops weirdly.

I look very inelegant arising from my slumber these days, huffing and swearing as I go. It's not a bad thing there's nobody but the dog there to see it.

What a body that wakes up in pain needs is a nice hot shower to uncurl a bit. However, going from prone, to upright, and then to a steamy shower is a *massive* gamble.

Many a morning I've taken to the shower (I mean, I don't like to go to work stinky) only to have to turn the water off and lie on the bathroom floor for a while. On a good day, if I'm not against the clock and I have plenty of time, I might not push myself so far up the Faint Scale and will catch myself at about a four, knowing I then have the opportunity to wrap myself in a towel and lie on my bed until I feel better.

But when I'm against the clock for such a thing as an early-morning PIP assessment, I have to try to limit the number of pit-stops. This means I might let myself get to a seven before I hurriedly stop and lie down naked on the cold linoleum bathroom floor… just in time. It can get a bit chilly in the winter.

You know those little wooden kids toys where the pieces of a puppet-type giraffe, or dog, or whatever are held together with elastic - and when you press in the big button on the bottom the animal suddenly collapses in a heap?

The *showering challenge* makes me feel like a giant one of those, and I don't quite know when some fucking sadist will press the button to make me go down. So I hurry up as best I can and hope to get through washing my bits, my face and my hair before they do.

On the plus side, if the conditioner has been left in my hair while I have a lie down, it feels lovely and soft afterwards!

I don't often actually faint, because I get plenty of warning and can usually take evasive action, but I do hit somewhere on my Faint Scale quite often. And the problem is *it's really fucking draining.* Did you know that the average human heart beats 115,600 times a day, while the average POTs patient's heart beats 345,600 times a day? *It's no wonder I'm always so bloody tired!*

So, here I am on the morning of my PIP assessment, and after one of those showers where I had to lie down three times (but I got up four!) I am bloody knackered before I even contemplate the fact that I have to get dressed and dry my hair. Understanding that a POTsy day is caused by dysautonomia, and that the autonomic system controls things like your bowel and bladder too, I could just tell this was going to be a delightful trip out.

◆

Having made it to the assessment center a pale, shaking mess, desperately needing the loo - from what I can tell, I have already proven myself ineligible to claim.

Yep, the very fact that I made it there at all seems to determine that I am too well to qualify.

First off, they are in the city center, not on a direct bus route, and they don't have a car park *(despite their sole purpose being to assess disabled clients - I mean what the holy hell?)*, so you have to park in a public car park just over 200 yards from their door - across a busy road. If you can find the car park by yourself and then walk from there, and get to their door without being killed by a car when crossing the busy road, you've already won yourself a big fat zero points for the mobility section.

Maybe it's deliberate, if they kill off a few applicants on the way they save a few quid, after all.

It doesn't matter if you found it difficult to plan your journey and you needed a Satnav and post-it notes, and still got lost on two roundabouts - you made it.

It doesn't matter if you got breathless, or if it'll take two weeks to get over the extra energy this excursion needed - you made it.

You HAVE to make it, because if you don't turn up for the assessment they won't process your application. But I can't see how anybody who makes it there gets approved, because they use your being able to get there against you! It's a conundrum.

Anyway there I was, and I soon found myself seated in a beige room in a rather *un*comfy chair across the desk from the assessor, who told me she was a nurse.

She came across as a kindly and sympathetic aunt, but if you have to go along for one of these things don't be fooled - they are not your friend. They will happily interrogate and trick you into what they would interpret as a confession that you are perfectly well and running marathons in your spare time.

I understand why they do this, particularly since there was a news article recently about a chap in his 70s who'd claimed not to be able to walk due to crippling arthritis but had in fact run two marathons that year, but it's hard for honest people like myself when the assessor's demeanour suggests *'You're all liars and I'm onto you!'*.

When asking if I could do simple tasks she wouldn't accept 'but it causes me pain', or 'but it causes me extreme fatigue' as answers - it was a simple yes or no situation as far as she was concerned, and I was not about to pretend I'm worse than I am.

'Can you raise your arms enough to get yourself dressed?'

'Yes, usually, but it hurts.'

'But you *CAN* do it, so *that's a yes!?*'

And so it went on…

People had told me they're slippery buggers and the only way to be understood was to exaggerate, and to only talk about my worst days (I told them I don't get out of bed on my worst days…) but look, the way I saw it was this: if I couldn't qualify truthfully, then I guess PIP wasn't designed for people like me…

If the house caught fire I would be able to get myself out of there – I'm sure I would get out of bed a bit quick (sod the stiff back) if I had to, so I guess I'm not really that immobile. I'm not so incapacitated that I'd have to just lie there and get barbequed.

So that was that.

I went home deflated, and absolutely exhausted. I'd had tears during the assessment - being made to think of all the worst aspects of your life for an hour will do that to you, especially when she asked how it affects Charlie and I had to think about the ways I fail him.

I barely got up over the next two days. I just didn't have the energy to lift myself from my bed after breaking my *pacing* routine with this additional, stressful trip out of the house.

But you're thinking it was probably worth it, right?

Well, it took around seven weeks to hear back - and of course I didn't get enough points to qualify. As we'd already worked out, the fact that I'd made it to the place at all meant that I scored a big fat zero for the 'mobility' section.

The report noted that I had some problems with 'daily living' and for those problems I scored a total of 6 points. You need 8 points minimum to receive the lowest level of support, so there would be no extra pennies for me.

I know some people don't take this sitting down (well, they do but you know what I mean) and they pursue their claim as far as a tribunal before they get what they deserve.

But the truth is I'd been a bit uncertain whether I deserved the help or not, so after a cursory 'reconsider request' came back with the same outcome, I took their word for it that I didn't.

After all PIP is a taxpayer-funded benefit and just because I'd paid tax myself for almost 30 years, I didn't take that lightly.

I have a lot of bad days of course, but I do have a few better days too, it's true. I imagined that when I was having a good day (which would usually be in the long school holidays when I can get plenty of rest), that I might risk getting the hose pipe out to wash down the car...

With my back brace strapped tight, my knee, ankle and wrist supports hidden under my clothes, and with it being the only physical task I'd try to get through all week so I could manage the fatigue, I'd know it wasn't an easy task. But these things need doing now and then (when you live by the coast you have seagulls to contend with, and we all know they're evil bastards and aim for our cars).

But I would be *mortified* to wake up one day and find my photo in the local journal, looking perfectly capable and being called a *benefits scrounger*.

It wouldn't matter that lots of planning and preparation went into things like this. All that would matter is that I could do it. The assessor's fairly stern *'so that's a yes'* was still ringing in my ears, after all.

And the photographic proof would be there...

And I honestly couldn't bear to be called a liar or a cheat - I honestly would rather starve!

Chapter 12

He Can't Help Being Called Kevin

I haven't seen allotment man for weeks. It's been really hot and his beloved plants are dead. I don't know why nobody is watering them for him - he always used to help people out and often teamed up to construct greenhouses with people, or held their beanpoles in place while they tried them together with string. It's made me a bit sad - not just seeing his plants die, but that the others haven't pulled together to look after things for him, for whatever reason he's not around. I can't believe he would just abandon everything - he was totally devoted!

I wonder if he's OK…

No, no I'm not still interested in seeing his marrow.

I can't say I'm interested in *anybody's* marrow right now, but I did have a brief flight of fancy about the new vet!

Oh yes, Kay loved this little episode - she so wants the Mills & Boon experience.

◆

I have to take Lillie to see the vet every two weeks - as if I don't have enough problems. Poor thing had bladder stones and they had to operate to scoop them all out. I'd never heard of dogs getting this before, but she had over 300 stones in there! Good god it's no wonder she kept waking me up at night to be let in the garden.

So, we go along every two weeks and they scan her bladder to make sure they aren't coming back. She's on super-expensive food now too, which is a necessary evil. She costs more to feed than my hollow-legged teenager, but it's not her fault.

The plus side of all this is that the vet is a bit of a dish. I know that's another saying that shows my age, but he is!

Lillie absolutely loves him and she starts getting excited when we pull into the car park. She jumps out of the car and drags me in like a loon, and when the vet comes out to see her she jumps all over him, tail wagging, as if she's totally forgotten that he regularly sticks needles in her. They have some strange kind of bond going on though, and he said, 'Her brain might not be too big, but she has a big heart to make up for it.'

Yes I know you're thinking *'they say dogs take after their owners'...*

I won't hold it against him that he's called Kevin. It's not a favourite name if I'm honest, not sure why - sorry to any other Kevins out there, but I couldn't imagine myself huskily calling out *'ooh Kevin'* in the throes of passion - just doesn't sound right does it? Maybe I knew a Kevin at school and didn't get on with him, I'm not sure...

Anyway, he makes up for it in other ways. He's probably a similar age to me, and he has the brightest blue eyes! He's got this casually floppy blonde hair, like he just doesn't care... *Oh shit, not in a Trump/Boris way - eww.*

It's just not over styled, like, he's not vain.

When he smiles this dimple appears in one cheek which is very endearing, and of course his chosen profession means he is clever - and nice. Who doesn't love an animal-lover?

It's not that I expect anything to come of it, but I do always pop a bit of fresh lip gloss on before we head in for an appointment.

Well, you would, wouldn't you?

I think Lillie would too, if I let her.

Will you think badly of me if I say I Facebook-searched him? He'd started to get quite chatty you see, and he was *fit*, so I just wanted to find out if he was single. Is that bad? I wasn't sure what I would do about it if he was but of course Kay was well up for me being the modern woman.

'You HAVE to ask him out, Lizzy. You absolutely have to. He'd be a great boyfriend!' she said.

'He already knows a bit about your problems and that hasn't stopped him being really nice to you!' Elle pointed out.

Ok, you might wonder how somebody who professes to be private about their health problems came to blurt them out to the dishy vet? Well, I'd had to mention the POTs when his little exam room was really hot and stuffy one day - there's no seating in there because of course you usually stand at the exam table with your pet perched up on it, so they can pop the thermometer where the sun don't shine without having to bend down. As he was explaining about *struvite crystals* and *urine density* I was starting to get a bit lightheaded.

Once my ears started to ring (a sign that all is not well), I briefly told him I have a tendency to faint and from then on he went above and beyond! He started to make the appointments for us outside of normal opening hours, when they didn't usually have people in so he could chat to me in the less stuffy reception area - with seats - instead of having to stand up in the small exam room.

He asked if I was managing to pay for all the appointments and I explained that the insurance had covered the op *(thank Christ!)* but the fortnightly scans came under monitoring, rather than treatment, which wasn't covered by the policy. And neither was the expensive prescription food, so I admitted that it was starting to be a bit of a stretch.

From then on he saw Lillie during his lunch break and didn't charge me unless we needed to send something like a blood test away, when I just had to pay the lab fees.

Now, I really wasn't sure how special this treatment was, and neither was I clear whether it was for my benefit, or because (as he'd said more than once) Lillie was his *favourite client.*

Of course Kay preferred to take the view that *I* was his favourite client and she was like the little devil on my shoulder talking me into the idea...

Given that I'd moved on from allotment man and it'd been years since I last dated, you can imagine that my lady bits were trying to get involved in the decision. A fit, thoughtful, generous vet, with lovely blue eyes and a cheeky dimple was being really quite nice to me.

I was bound to try to find out if he was single, *right?*

Well he wasn't.

Of course.

The good ones never are, are they?

So it was the dog he had a soft spot for, and not her daft owner…

I know, if this was any kind of decent rom-com he would not only have been single, but he'd have fancied me back and been secretly hoping I'd ask him out. Sorry to let you down, folks, but as you know my life has been significantly more shit than your typical rom-com.

Oh well. It was a nice thought while it lasted wasn't it?

Chapter 13

Who's She?

I saw a thing on Pinterest a while ago that said 'I don't always get ill, but when I do, it's probably with something you've never heard of.'

OK, I do often get ill, but the thing about *something you've never heard of* strikes home. Here's the latest.

I went back to my GP and asked if he really thought POTs and fibro explained my problems. I'd had one appointment with the POTs people when they tested and diagnosed on the same day, and one private meeting with a Doctor who diagnosed fibro, but there was no ongoing care or support for these things. I was given a label, the pills, and sent on my way.

I'd already explained the good, the bad and the ugly with the Gabapentin (I still got The Shits, unfortunately - I never went anywhere without a supply of Imodium) and he sat back in his chair and looked at me.

I stopped talking.

He stopped talking.

It was a tad disconcerting.

'Have you heard of Ehlers Danlos?' He asked.

'No, who's she?'

'It's something I'm just wondering about. It's not very common, but I read something about it recently and it could explain your problems. How would you feel about me sending you to see an EDS specialist? There's a Consultant in Bristol who is also a POTs specialist because the two conditions often go together,' he offered.

Alrighty then...

It took about 8 weeks for the appointment to come through, not bad at all for an in-demand specialist, during which time I was asked to write a *top to toe* list of my ailments.

Blimey.

I won't lie, I've become a bit if a wuss these days and the idea of getting myself an hour or so up the road to Bristol wasn't fun, you know how I am with mornings, and trips out. But I'm not daft and I know how valuable this appointment is. When the day came around I gritted my teeth, got in the car and made it there with the help of my Satnav an hour early. I absolutely hate being late for anything so I always leave way too much time, which also allows for regular loo stops if my guts are in a bad way too.

It's really strange that after decades of being rushed through ten minute appointments with Doctors whose shoulders visibly sagged when they saw I was next, only to come away feeling that I was being written off as a time-waster, that this experience - of being before a specialist who not only smiled at me, but nodded when I explained things, asked questions and listened to the replies, (even pre-empting what I was going to say), and who had a cheerful attitude - was *fucking extraordinary!*

He didn't break eye contact when I explained things - he didn't look at his screen and start typing the standard 'depressed' line on my notes before I even had the first words out of my mouth. He didn't rush me. He nodded and said, *'Oh, that's making life difficult, isn't it?'*

He was understanding, but, well... *jolly.* This meant we got through a whole lot of shit without me really noticing!

And I didn't cry!

After a long chat he placed me in the care of some nurses who did blood tests and an 'active stand test' (a poor man's tilt table test, essentially - the same thing as I had before, but you just stand up instead of using the special - and no doubt expensive - tilt table). Then at the end of the appointment and with no long wait for a typed letter to arrive via the GP, he sat me down and said that he did indeed think that I had both POTs AND hEDS.

There are different types of EDS and mine was the most common and least problematic - the main characteristic is hypermobile joints.

It's a strange thing, after so many years (did I say that I'm 46 now), to hear that you have *something.* It almost made me giggle. An odd reaction I know, so I managed to hold it in, as that would be quite inappropriate, even for a nice-natured Doctor.

It's perhaps time for another blue box, do you think?

Again feel free to skip it!

◆

Hypermobile Ehlers-Danlos syndrome is an inherited connective tissue disorder that is caused by defects in a protein called collagen. It is generally considered the least severe form of Ehlers-Danlos syndrome (EDS) although significant complications can occur.

Although hypermobile EDS is thought to be a genetic condition, the exact underlying cause is unknown in most cases. A small percentage of people with this condition have a mutation in the TNXB gene. Treatment and management is focused on preventing serious complications and relieving associated signs and symptoms.

The signs and symptoms of hypermobile Ehlers-Danlos syndrome vary but may include:

- Joint hypermobility affecting both large and small joints
- Frequent joint dislocations and subluxations (partial dislocation), often affecting the shoulder, kneecap, and/or temporomandibular joint
- Soft, smooth skin that may be slightly elastic and bruises easily.
- Chronic musculoskeletal pain
- Early-onset osteoarthritis.
- Osteoporosis
- Gastrointestinal issues such as nausea, vomiting, heartburn, constipation, or hiatal hernia
- Dysfunction of the autonomic nervous system
- Cardiovascular abnormalities such as mitral valve prolapse or aortic root dilatation
- Pregnancy complications

Symptoms can include but are not limited to: sleep disturbance (tick), fatigue (tick), postural orthostatic tachycardia (tick), functional gastrointestinal disorders (tick), dysautonomia (tick), anxiety, and depression *(ha! - don't tell my old Drs they could've been right to think I may have been sad!!).*

◆

Ok, so that's the generic info.

But what this means for me is that I have an actual reason for the things people had come to think I was making up!

Jesus Christ - it was, well everything!

I have to tell you something funny. When the specialist asked if I had a partner at home I explained that no, I have been single for quite a few years now. He pulled a sympathetic face and I thought he was about to say it was a shame I didn't have somebody else at home to share the chores or look after me a bit when I had bad days, but no.

'Have you heard that you can get sex robots now?' he said.

Can you believe it?!

At least he didn't offer to model me a dildo, I suppose!

Chapter 14

The Power Of Facebook

You'll often hear the medical profession tell you that you should **absolutely not** google your symptoms (even though I have seen my Drs do this more than once!), but in this case he actually advised me to look up EDS to get a better understanding of it.

I wasn't freaking out about it or anything - for crying out loud I knew people who'd walked into their Doctor's and been given the worst possible news, and I'd been to enough funerals to know things could be very much worse. This wasn't going to stop me from remaining on the planet to look after my boy while he needed me, so I knew I was lucky. But I guess armed with information and a decent understanding I could figure out ways to help myself as much as possible.

So, I found another Facebook group, and learned a bit more about this relatively rare condition. Even though it varies greatly from person to person there's enough common ground to show me I'm not alone. Having felt a bit like a fucking freak most of my life you can imagine this is extremely comforting.

Having a new 'label' doesn't change the fact that I prefer to keep myself to myself - I'm not about to buy the T-shirt, I'm afraid. No car bumper sticker for me...

I know people do like to raise awareness and I do admire them for it, but I'm just not that way inclined.

A handful of people had kept up with my appointment news and would be told the outcome. Mum of course, who seemed totally unconcerned (she's in her 80s and I try not to worry her - but then I get conflicted as I do such a good job of that she becomes blasé about it all when really I wouldn't mind a touch of the *there there's* - after all that's what mums are for!). The girls, who were also led by my lack of worry, and of course my sister.

I have an amazing relationship with my big sister Jane - she's the absolute best. We look nothing alike. In fact when she was younger she looked rather Chinese, as opposed to my somewhat Celtic complexion, but she looks like mum and I look like dad so I don't think we need to ask too many questions.

When I was about 13 I think, she'd not long passed her driving test and I had to go to the dentist to have some teeth taken out. I now know that dental overcrowding is a common thing for people with EDS and I had to have ten teeth pulled.

In those days they used some kind of foul smelling and rank tasting gas to put you to sleep at the dentist. I think they stopped doing this because there were too many fatalities! These days kids go to hospital, but they popped the mask on me and off I went.

I have fuzzy memories of much of my childhood but by Christ I remember this well enough.

As does my poor sister.

My recollection is of a very surreal dream - that stuff must really fuck with your mind. I was in an endless white space and I could hear this constant high pitched tone.

And I was spinning.

I don't mean turning like I was dancing, I mean I was at the end of some long-armed 'thing' which was also white like everything else I could see, being spun around, and around, and around with frightening velocity, and there was all this bright white space, and this blinding white light that I kept spinning past, and this tone kept ringing...

My sister's recollection is the shit-scary responsibility of being called in by the local GP, who had attended the appointment to administer the gas anaesthetic, because he couldn't wake me up. I don't remember this bit of course but they were calling me, and slapping my face, and shaking me - and I wouldn't respond.

I mean, I must've been alive! I am sure they'd have called an ambulance and not just my teenage sister if I'd stopped breathing, but I clearly was either being really, really lazy or I just could not get off the spinney thing and come back.

Freaky stuff.

Poor Jane was told to come in and *speak sternly* to me to get me to wake up.

Anyway, this is how *there for me* my sister has always been. I have been lucky enough to return the favour now and then - she has occasionally needed me, too. But those are her stories to tell, not mine, so I'll leave that there.

◆

'I want more for you Lizzy, you deserve to have a fuller life,' she said, while I tried to brush off her concern along with the cake crumbs that had landed on the coffee table. She'd come over to help me put together a waist-height veg trug I'd bought online so I could do some planting in the garden without hurting my back. Job done (we were a good team) we'd stopped for coffee and some of the home-made lemon drizzle cake she'd bought with her.

'What can we do to give you back more of your life? You shouldn't be scared to go out in case you faint, you should be enjoying your life like most people your age,' she said.

Gulp.

It's funny how I can have these chats with the girls, and moments later we'll be laughing about something stupid. With my sister saying this, it did hit home a bit more. I was determined not to cry - this was an almost unheard of occurrence reserved for professionals - but she was certainly tugging at the heart strings. Maybe it was because many of the best experiences of my life had been shared with her.

Pre-Charlie, we and our then husbands usually went on our holidays together as a foursome. But while she's continued to enjoy her travels, I'm not making any more memories. Mine are limited to the ones I've already made.

I can't afford to travel these days since I don't work full time, even if I had the confidence that my health would allow me to enjoy it. But I'm grateful that I'd got to see some places on my list before things went to shit.

I've been to Paris, Rome, Pisa, Naples, New York...

We had some fun cycling holidays in France, although Jane recently reminded me that I was always bringing up the rear - the others waiting ahead calling 'come on Lizzy!' as I peddled, red faced and heart racing, to catch up. As soon as I'd catch up the evil bastards would start peddling again, so I'd never get the rest stops that they did!

We also enjoyed interesting sightseeing in the Florentine museums, and toured Pompeii and Herculaneum. We had an amazing holiday in Sorrento, where we visited the foreigners bar, and watched an impressive lightning storm over Mt. Vesuvius from the comfort of our hotel balcony.

We visited the colosseum and saw the Roman mosaics in Tunis, much better preserved than the one in Rome (although their gelato is better), and we drank wine under the same sunshine the grapes were grown under. We had some relaxing 'pool & Kindle' holidays in the Canary Islands, and endured a less pleasant stay in Egypt where we were discouraged from leaving the hotel by gun-wielding security.

And, along with our respective husbands, she was always there. Sharing the good times, making the memories, and keeping a little bit of a protective eye on me.

I fucking hated airports - you know they are queue, after queue, after queue. And inevitably hot - especially at the other end.

But when you travel in a small group of responsible adults that can be managed. I would sit on the floor or pace around and re-join them in the queue as it shuffled along.

While we were out and about I was always a little more tired than the others, often needed a longer siesta, and of course the Polymorphic Light Eruption (sun allergy) had to be managed, but we cheerfully ignored all of that and had some bloody fantastic times.

There are lots of places I haven't been though, and there are a lot of things I haven't done. I can't say it's always easy seeing others go on ahead. She works hard and is very deserving of her holidays, but comparing us these days highlights many more differences than it does likenesses, and that's when I see things through her eyes.

I think she would feel better if I had a special someone - and that's almost a big enough reason to try, just so she wouldn't feel so worried about me. But now that my dating profile would be more POTs and EDS than GSOH and SWF that's looking less likely than ever.

I know she worries that I'm becoming reclusive, but I don't really feel as much empty space in my life as people might think. For a start, when you sleep a lot of the weekend away there's less time to fill. And of course I still have Charlie - as much as any parent has their teenager for company.

I've joined several Facebook support groups too, which fill my news feed, and while I don't manage to meet up with the girls so often these days, we have a group chat which pings often enough to make sure I'm never truly lonely.

So no, I'm not too alone - I have Charlie, the girls, my mum, my sister/best friend, and apparently I have my Angel.

Yes, you heard me right...

Chapter 15

Everybody Needs Good Neighbours

Let me tell you about my neighbour.

Beverley moved here at the same time as we did - into one of the nicer cream-coloured houses. Her grown-up sons had flown the nest, she was single, and she'd downsized to save money as she wasn't earning a great deal as a psychic.

Yep!

You can phone her from one of those online directories for psychics. She wears a headset as she goes about her business at home, and when the phone rings she will give the caller a *telephone reading.*

At least it's not a sex line, I'm not sure I could cope with hearing those kinds of calls through the open window.

I'm not going to give away whether I believe in all this or not, but the point is, she does. I've been uneasy in the past about people paying for this type of thing - I'm sure a 20 minute call is not that cheap (with most of the money going to the internet promoters) but I can't say she's a charlatan when she wholeheartedly believes in her powers. She is guided either by her angelic cards (like tarot cards), her crystal collection, or by her Archangel.

She asks him to help open her third eye to offer love and light to help her to heal people.

She is very kind, and often picks up on the fact that, say, my back is particularly painful one day. She'll sometimes pick this up without seeing me - just through the adjoining wall, I guess - and she'll text me to ask about it. If I let on that she's right she'll either meet me at the garden fence to pass over a homeopathic remedy, or she'll offer to send me some *healing.*

Her remedies aren't like painkillers, of course - they don't treat the symptom like conventional drugs. They treat the psychological or emotional reason you have the pain in the first place. She tells me my back pain, since it radiates through my right hip, is because a man is 'hooked' into me. She says she can unhook him and send him on his way, but unless he unhooks his end as well the pain might come back.

See, I knew men were a pain in the arse.

She went so far the other day as to say the reason I have poor health is that I am psychotic (I think she has more in common with modern medicine that she cares to believe!). She said that although I appear calm, balanced, and very kind, that deep down my family has a psychotic trait, and managing that has caused my physical illness.

Who am I to say she's not right?!

She looks exactly as you would expect her to - she has cropped 'elfin' like hair and wears all natural, floaty linen clothes. She wears crystals around her neck and her pristine house smells of aromatherapy oils and incense.

She makes her own organic, chemical-free deodorant, and has a weekly delivery of farm-fresh organic vegetables.

She has a shaggy black cat whose pictures she posts on Facebook, and who Lillie barks at through the fence.

Putting her beliefs aside - you can make your own mind up about those - she is also thoughtful. If I've left my wheelie-bin out she'll perhaps realise it's because I'm not feeling great and will drag it back in for me. She passes bunches of flowers, or sometimes a new remedy she's just mixed up over the garden fence now and then.

She came and sat in my garden with me one afternoon and asked if she could practice her hand massage technique for a spirit fair she was going to. I'm sure she was just being nice and offering me a relaxing treatment for free, because I *know* I was looking like utter shit that day. She's the only person besides Charlie who has to see me without my face on – I'm hardly going to bother just to put the laundry out to dry.

She drove me to have my cortisone injection in my ankle, too. I usually prefer to go to appointments alone so I don't have to be sociable while concentrating on managing my issues, but since it was my clutch foot and I don't have an automatic car I conceded to a lift this time. Knowing that my sister works full time, she'd volunteered as soon as she worked out that I wouldn't be able to drive myself.

I've helped her out, too. She's not too practical and when we moved in she had no idea how to do things like put a loo roll holder up, and she didn't understand how the boiler worked so I popped in a few times to explain what to do until she'd figured it out - that kind of thing.

She adores Charlie.

The main reason is that he's extremely considerate of our neighbours, well aware that we're in a terraced house, and she never hears a peep out of him.

He wears headphones so we can't hear his gaming noises, unlike some teenagers who play war games so loud the neighbours must get PTSD, and he walks quietly around the house instead of tearing around. He's just not the door-slamming type.

Given that Beverley spends a lot of time in complete silence waiting for the next phone call, either painting in *healing therapy colours* or making little felt angels to sell on her website, she would certainly notice if he was yelling or blasting music out. So she feels very lucky that we don't disturb her quiet chats with her angels.

She tells me I have an archangel too, but he can't help me unless I specifically ask him to...

There are plenty of people who are helped by people like Beverley, and you may be one of them so you won't find me telling you it's a load of bollocks. There's a current trend among celebs for crystal healing and if it's good enough for Victoria Beckham who am I to say it doesn't work? We all find our own ways through life, and she's not hurting anybody.

The point is, it's nice to have a neighbour who cares. It could be much worse, after all.

It's only recently that I found out the reason mum said I could pack in my paper round all those years ago was less about my fainting and more about our pervy neighbour at the time, who'd signed up to have a newspaper delivered just so I'd have to open his gate and walk up his drive, while apparently he stood proud - and completely starkers - at his bedroom window.

He did this while the kids were walking past on their way home from the nearby primary school too, so mum got together with a few of the others mums and told the police. He was charged and mum had to go to court to give evidence.

The funny thing is I'd never even noticed!!

So yes, I'd much rather have a neighbour like Beverley than that fat old perv.

Chapter 16

The Fog Has Lifted

I had a routine (3-monthly) appointment with the specialist in Bristol recently. No talk of sex robots again, I'm happy to report.

One of the things we spoke about was the loathsome fatigue. This was the most life-limiting aspect of my diagnoses and I had no idea how to improve the situation. He asked me more about my sleep, and one question he asked reminded me of a shit-scary night when I'd stayed at my sister's house a few years ago.

I was fairly newly single at the time and Charlie had been with his dad, so she'd invited me over for take-away and a chilled night in front of the TV. Rather than head out into the cold night afterwards, she'd suggested I should crash in her spare room and go home after breakfast.

She probably wished she'd never suggested it, as I ended up running into her room, incoherent and crying at about 3am. I'm a pretty calm and rational person but I'd been woken up *by a ghost!*

I'd been lying on my back half awake, half asleep. My eyes were open and I could see this dark presence in the room, which soon started to *loom* over me. After a short time I felt a heavy pressure on my chest - I tried to move, but I was completely pinned down and could hardly breathe.

I tried to fight it off and shout at it to leave me alone, but it was too strong and I just couldn't move, nor could I find my voice. In my head I was screaming as loud as I could, but I couldn't hear the sound so I knew it wasn't filling the room. The next thing I knew I was being lifted slightly from the bed and thrown roughly back down.

And then it was gone.

It was a moment or two before I could move and it was completely terrifying. I'd had a brief thought that it was my dad coming back to tell me off for getting divorced, but I'm sure he'd have found a kinder way to get his message across. I have probably never been so scared in my life and once I could move I had to leave the room - of course I ran to find Jane to tell her about being attacked by a ghost in her spare bed.

She managed not to laugh at me, and after calming me down she sent me back to bed, where I lay awake with the light on, counting the delicate flowers on the curtains until the morning.

Of course in the cold light of day I realised it wasn't *actually* a ghost. Even with my rational head on it wasn't easy to shake off the feeling of utter terror, but we worked out it had probably been sleep paralysis, possibly brought on by divorce-related stress. It happened again, more than once, but the next time I didn't panic quite so much.

I also have really lucid, full colour dreams, and I've often thought that if only I could hold onto the details for long enough I could write a good book based on some of the complex plots, but they vanish as soon as I open my eyes...

The consultant asked me if I'd ever experienced problems like sleep apnoea, sleep paralysis and vivid dreams, and it seems it's a common feature of dysautonomia. He couldn't exactly say why that is, but it's probably to do with poor quality of sleep. Disturbances during REM sleep can have a pretty drastic effect - it's literally the stuff of nightmares.

It turns out that the entire scenario is really common with sleep paralysis, from the dark presence in the room, to the heavy weight suffocating the dreamer. Some cultures say its devilish creatures coming to get you in the night - I honestly have no idea how they ever get their kids to go to bed.

◆

We also discussed my Gabapentin *brain fog.* In a recent episode of Elementary, Sherlock was put on Gabapentin for severe headaches and even he lost his sharp mental edge and powers of deduction, so that made me feel a bit better. But there have been a few new reports about Gabapentin recently, saying it's the new Valium scandal waiting to happen. They say it is highly addictive.

I feel sorry for people who need it to control their epilepsy - those people have no choice - but it seems it's being overused *off label* and people are being now warned about it. Although knowing the Daily Mail it'll be really good for you again this time next week.

Anyway, he reckons it's not the right drug for me to be taking, and likely isn't helping my chronic fatigue.

He told me to wean off it slowly, over a few months. It's quite dangerous to come off it fast, and I know from the odd occasion when I forgot to take a dose that when you do stop it makes you feel absolutely goddamn awful. It's not just a return of the old symptoms - you go through actual withdrawal.

Something to look forward to.

I planned to reduce the dose when I knew I would be at home for a few days with ready access to the loo. It'd had that kind of effect when I was late with a dose, so I was dreading to think how it would affect me as I was cutting down properly. And I was right to be concerned - every time I cut down a bit more I felt like I was an extra in Trainspotting. It wasn't a happy time, but after a couple of months I was fully off it. The good news is - the fog has lifted! I can already feel myself starting to be able to think again! I mean, I hurt like hell, but you can't have everything...

Now I was off that shit completely I could start with some new drugs. He prescribed Midodrine, which is a vasoconstrictor so it helps people with POTs, and (unable to prescribe it in the UK yet) he told me to research CBD oil. He gave me a couple of websites to review and said other patients had reported some success with it. I was reassured to find it was the legal, over-the-counter type he was suggesting, and not the kind that gets you high (or arrested), so after some research I placed an order.

Mum was unsure - all she could think was *'but its cannabis!'* but she didn't freak out too much.

I think she had a brief vision of me in dreadlocks wearing a red, gold and green tie-dye T-shirt and wondered how she'd explain it all to her posh friends at the W.I.

My neighbour approved as it's essentially just an extreme herbal remedy. After giving me some crystals to pop inside my bra, *'They'll give you energy,'* she also decided to order some CBD oil for herself.

Chapter 17

Magic Hands

I managed to shave my legs this morning, AND put my face on. I am leaving the house for something other than work, which is a bit of an event these days.

Sorry, no it's not a date. It is an *appointment*.

I have been referred to a 'Wellbeing Hub', which I am extremely fortunate to have just up the road from where I live. It used to be a local hospital but cutbacks meant that was closed down a couple of years ago, but it's still an NHS facility and they have a physio/rehab type area alongside an audiologist, a podiatrist, a little gym and even a cafe. It's mostly aimed at the elderly community I think but who am I to complain.

I've been referred for physio/pain management.

I still have some pride, so knowing I was being physically assessed I sat down in the empty bath (tap running but no plug in) and dragged a razor over my pale freckly shins, turning the shower on afterwards for a rinse. *Go me!*

I donned the sportswear I haven't dug out of the bottom of my drawer for years and off I went. A non-scary two minute drive got me there comfortably and I found my way along the windy corridors and up the stairs to the physio waiting area.

It's August, and it's the hottest summer we've had since 1976. Heat is not my friend and I sat there with my traditional bamboo and paper fan (I don't care if I look daft) gathering myself before my name was called. I was a little POTsy - sometimes even if I haven't escalated up the Faint Scale I can visibly tremble, and this was one of those days, but I was doing OK.

'Lizzy?'

I looked up and saw a familiar face - and it grinned the widest grin back at me.

'Hi Lizzy, it's me Chris. Good to see you again!'

'Hi, Chris.'

So, that was unexpected.

The last time I'd seen Chris was at the physio unit in our neighbouring town, but it seems he works here a few days a week, too.

And of all the things I thought would happen today, getting a *spark* from bumping into Chris again was not on the list. I didn't remember that from last time... maybe it was just because I was a bit POTsy today.

So I fanned myself a little faster and followed him into our little curtained area. It's all shiny and new - it's actually a great place.

'So, Lizzy - how've you been?' he asked.

Christ, is he ready for this?

He sat down with his notepad and I began to explain about the EDS and POTs diagnoses I'd had since I saw him last time, keeping any references about getting the shits to myself, and explained that the back problem he'd started to help me with was just a part of the overall problem.

He had a little pre-printed drawing of a man on his clipboard, and as his pen hovered over the blank outline he asked me to explain my problem areas. What they do is roughly colour in the areas you say are painful, so a patient might go in with left knee pain and they'd scribble that part of the little man in. Ha!

Basically he coloured the whole little outline man in, piece by piece, as I told him about this problem, and that pain… it was like the opposite of a date, where you might highlight your best features. Here I was explaining all my worst as if I was reading out my shopping list.

'Quite a lot going on there!' he said.

'What do you hope for? What would you most like to achieve out of these sessions?' he asked.

'I'd quite like to get laid,' obviously didn't leave my mouth - thank goodness the Gabapentin brain fog has gone and I have control over what I say again.

'Well, if I can get more mobile, maybe I'll have more energy to walk my dog again. Then maybe I'll get a bit fitter and be able to lose some of the weight I put on when I was taking Gabapentin,' I replied.

That's better.

Chris decided to start with the worst issue first and delved a bit more into the lower back and hip pain. He got me to lie on my back on the shiny, teal, plastic-coated bed and gently took hold of my leg (see I knew I was right to get the razor out!) and he started manoeuvring me about, feeling into my hip to see what was going on in there. Now I know I was going red - and not just because no man has laid his hands on me for a very long time, but because this was not exactly pain-free.

He got me to lie on my front. I managed to turn over without swearing.

'The muscles in your back are really tight,' he said before pushing around a bit to *make some adjustments.*

'Argh!! *No shit!*'

He got me to stand up and held out his hands for support while he asked me to go through a range of motions, which reminded me I'd had no right to be smug during my childhood ballet lessons. Here I was 40 something years later wobbling around with my tongue out just to balance on one leg, then to go up onto my toes and back down again. I was rather pleased he was supporting me and I was doing quite well to ignore the little *frisson* of - something.

What the hell?

From what you know about EDS by now you probably think I'm really flexible, so when he asked me to bend forwards and touch my toes I'd do it no sweat, right?

But that was before.

146

That was when I was younger, and yes hypermobility was great for my sex life back in the day! (Except I've always had quite bad Temporomandibular Joint (TMJ) syndrome - also common in EDS, I gather - so anything that involved the jaw was off the table...)

Hypermobility causes joint damage and painful muscle tightening, so by my age the floor is a very long way away.

After a little more unintentional torture he let me relax. Although I was secretly wincing at the pain, having just had a few of my worst spots poked at.

'You ok?' he asked.

'Yep...'

Actually my hip felt like he'd stabbed me with a hot poker.

Here's what I know since Chris gave me a little biology lesson: When connective tissue doesn't do its job at holding your skeleton together, your muscles have to take over as best they can. Not only does this cause them pain, and fatigue from being overworked, but they weren't really hired for the job and they haven't had the training, so they don't really do it right. This is why my lower spine was going for a little sideways stroll. There might also be Ankylosing Spondylitis (arthritis stiffening) in my lower back too, but that would only be confirmed with an X-ray, and frankly I've had enough radiation exposure in my lifetime not to bother.

My hip pain and sciatica is most likely Piriformis Syndrome - the piriformis muscle in my bum cheek loves my sciatic nerve so much it hugs it with all its might.

Not only is the muscle irritation painful (in a deep, burning way) but compressing the nerve like this makes the pain and heat travel down my leg. By day this is bloody painful, by night my right leg kind of fizzes, like there's loads of little electric shocks going on in there. It seems like once you get this it never quite goes away and I can attest to that after at least a decade of this bothersome affliction, but perhaps Chris can now teach me how to help it a bit.

He brought out a model of the spine and told me the role of the different parts, where the connective tissue gets involved, and why there is pain when things go wrong.

Nobody had ever really explained this stuff to me before.

Then he gave me just four exercises to go away and try at home, with a follow up due in a fortnight to see how I was getting on. He basically told me I have to stop protecting myself so much, and to down the painkillers to break the pain cycle enough to get moving again, so that I could hopefully improve the longer-term outlook.

Then he smiled at me like he hadn't just tortured me and said, 'See you in two weeks!'

What the fuck just happened?

◆

Now, since I'd never got around to the idea of a sex robot, you can imagine that this fit, hipster physio, who was tall, athletic, knowledgeable, and with a clear sense of fun (as he allowed me not to be too serious again during our 45 minute session) had somehow pressed a few buttons.

I have absolutely no idea how old he is but I'm worried that he's much younger - not because I think that would put him off me because there's no reason at all to think that he would ever be *on* me. But because it would feel even more wrong to have reacted like this if he was. I just don't see myself as cougar material.

The problem is the last decade has flashed by in such a blur (particularly the Gabapentin years) it's almost like it never happened, and I kind of forget I'm no longer in my (late) 30s! Everyone tells me I look younger too, possibly down to a lifetime of sun avoidance (and Elemis marine cream), and when I look at men my age they look... *flipping old.*

Even Charlie's dad was looking every bit his nearly 50 years old these days. So I told myself off and decided I was probably perving over someone at least a decade younger than I was, who would never look twice at a broken, middle aged, single mum - and focussed on ignoring the pain during the daily exercise routine he gave me.

Good god I really do need to get out more...

Chapter 18

All Too Familiar

We've already discussed the fact that thanks to my physical limitations I am not mum of the year. But it gets worse.

When you find out - after having a child - that you have a potentially inherited condition, what's your biggest fear?

Indeed.

Charlie, who is now a full head taller than me, has been coming over faint at school. His best friend relayed this to me and it turns out Charlie hadn't mentioned it so he wouldn't make a fuss, but she was worried about him and wanted me to know.

I wonder who he takes after...

Of course he was also sleeping a lot more, and at weekends I'd be lucky to see him before 3pm, but I'm well aware that most teenagers do this so I wasn't jumping to any conclusions. If I was having a good day at the weekend I'd try and follow Chris's advice and go for a brief walk with the dog and I'd started to drag Charlie with me to get him away from his screen for 20 minutes, but I'd noticed he seemed to tire as much as I did after just walking a flat mile.

Hmmm typical teenage stuff or something more, I wonder?

He also desperately hated PE and I'd always thought it was because he spends too much time at his desk and is seriously unfit, but it seems to be more than that. His heart races and he says his legs really ache.

A while ago I put my head around his bedroom door to check in on him, 'All ok in Charlie's world?' I asked. He smiled back and gave me his trademark thumbs up. I noticed that his digit curled right back on itself.

A little alarm bell started to ring, so when he was at a convenient point in his gaming (you can't just ask a teen to stop gaming immediately because if they leave a competitive match before it's finished they get banned for a few days, which is absolutely the end of the world) I asked him to come and chat with me.

He sat down and I asked him to tell me a bit more about the times he's felt faint at school. I'm a really calm person - I wasn't sitting him down with a spotlight in his eyes interrogating him or anything, and I was careful not to put words in his mouth. I just said I needed to understand what was happening so we could think about whether it was something we needed to deal with. It turns out it's times like standing outside the classroom in the corridor waiting to be allowed into lessons.

I then asked him to show me some moves - I knew how the Beighton Score worked by now so I got him to try the positions.

Shit.

Finally, I have an Oximeter at home - a little device (cheap as chips from Amazon) that you pop on your finger.

It shows your heart rate and oxygen levels in real time, so it's much more accurate than an exercise monitor like a Fitbit. Over the next few days we did a few active stand tests with the Oximeter to see if he was showing signs of orthostatic intolerance. For teenagers, the threshold is slightly different - the heart rate from sitting to standing has to raise by 40 bmp or more to be considered POTsy (it's 30 bmp in adults).

He was routinely hitting the high 30s and once or twice went over the 40s. His legs looked like corned beef, too.

Fuckadoodledoo.

My lovely POTs/EDS consultant has always been very open to receiving emails - and he answers them (himself, not just asking an assistant or whatever to do it!) so I emailed him to ask about Charlie. He's not a paediatrician so he wouldn't usually see under 18s, but he did say that at 14 years old he was probably 'about adult sized' so he would make an exception and see him.

Off we trundled for our afternoon out and bless him Charlie was really calm about the whole thing. It's not nice knowing you're going into a hospital for tests, even if you know they aren't going to be painful or anything, but he really held it together.

It was actually quite nice having the time in the car together since I don't get much quality time with him these days. The times when he'd wake up at 6am and crawl into my bed for a snuggle are of course long gone.

Our lovely consultant asked Charlie a familiar bunch of questions then took him through the Beighton test routine before sending him off for a proper active stand test.

As it happened, Charlie was having a good day - his heart rate didn't rise above 40 bpm and he didn't go ghostly pale as he sometimes does (which feels all too familiar, unfortunately).

As he did with me, the consultant looked at all the results at the same appointment and called us back in for the verdict. He concluded that Charlie was on the 'hypermobile spectrum' but didn't quite meet the criteria for hEDS.

He also said he showed some orthostatic intolerance but didn't quite meet the criteria for POTs.

Good news - ish.

It would obviously have been significantly better news had he not shown any signs of anything, but the fact that he was not as badly off as I was could only be good. He also said that he could be exhibiting a sort of adolescent orthostatic intolerance due to his rapid growth spurt and that he may grow out of it.

Here's hoping.

It also explains his god awful handwriting!

He's always getting teacher comments about his writing being too hard to read.

It doesn't help that he's left handed and if he hasn't got the right pen in his bag the ink smudges everywhere, but now I know that his complaints about getting really achy hands after a few minutes of writing are genuine and not just because he hates English (he's more of a Maths whizz). Hypermobility *does* make your hands get achy and tired really easily.

At primary school I recall they allowed him to use a laptop more often - they said he always had great ideas but struggled to get them down on paper, and they'd rather find out what he has to say than know that he's truncated his ideas. In hindsight I'd wondered if that early lack of handwriting practice had made the problem worse, but now I know it is a genuine problem.

I might have to speak to school - he's just starting his GCSE years and will have to face sit-down exams soon. I wonder if there is anything we can do...

We got the usual advice about more salt and more water along with some tips about *blood pumping* to help ease the symptoms if they start coming on.

Again there was no mention of sex robots, which is good, as a 14 year old lad might quite like the idea...

Chapter 19

Pain In The Bum

I've had a busy few weeks - mum needed taking to hospital for some tests, Charlie needed the orthodontist (he's inherited the dental overcrowding as well, unfortunately) and of course Lillie needed her regular scan at the vet. Work has been quite busy too - the chap I share an office with says I'm too nice and should learn to say no, but if somebody asks for my help I always brightly say, *'Of course!'*

I suppose I never quite got over the desire to feel useful to somebody…

So I'm knackered, but I've done my best to do the physio homework Chris set for me. One of the moves is bloody painful and I've had to reach for the painkillers more often - the CBD oil doesn't touch it, but I've persevered - I can't let him down, can I?

And so here I am, sat in the empty bath dragging a razor over my goose-bumpy legs again.

◆

Chris called me in - flashing me his usual grin - and asked me to show him how I'd been getting on. I was keen to prove I'd been trying and wasn't wasting the help I was being given, and he was pleased to see I'd made some progress. I could now stand up from my chair without huffing or hauling myself up with my hands.

Oh yes, I was hands-free standing.

Perhaps not an Olympic sport, but it was something.

The muscle in my bum was still really painful though, and I was unsure how to bring up this delicate matter, but it had to be done and when Chris poked around and found the spot, I managed not to smack him.

He gave me a few more exercises to try at home. He explained a sideways leg lift that would target my *gluteus medius* and asked me to do ten reps. I'd have done that no sweat a few years ago but Jesus Christ, it was bloody agony! My leg was wobbling and trembling all over the shop. I hadn't really realised how little control I had over it, but we laughed and he said maybe we'd go for 5 a day for now.

Since starting the Midodrine I have to say I'm not properly POTsy so often, and since I worry a lot about *deconditioning* I've managed to push myself to walk the dog quite a few times now!

Chris suggested I keep that up, as long as I could manage it without causing too much fatigue it would obviously help my aches and pains much more than days spent lying on the sofa. I was some way off releasing the dog walker from her duties, but a little flat stroll now and then would be a decent target for now.

I've had a heart scan recently too, which is routine for EDSers as they sometimes have heart valve problems. I'd forgotten that a previous Doctor thought she'd heard a murmur and I wasn't worried – after all it was just to rule things out.

I was a touch more worried when the scan was carried out by a young man. I'd expected a female would do it since it's rather personal (I mean, they are probing around by your exposed boobs), but Christ knows I've had worse. The same locum GP who'd mentioned the murmur had also carried out a smear test, and had looked up from between my legs to say, *'Oh dear, that doesn't look right at all!'* which put the shits up me a bit.

I'd always had *women's problems*, but that was a small fire issue until she referred me to the oncology unit for an urgent colposcopy. This was again carried out by a male specialist - which was significantly worse than having my boobs prodded by a hard, slimy probe. Everything turned out to be OK. Well, something wasn't *quite* right, but I won't go into gory details and it was nothing to cause ongoing concern.

The heart scan results came back via my Bristol Doctor, and it seems they found a small Atrial Septal Defect (ASD), but that it wasn't particularly *hemodynamically significant.* Basically it wasn't a heart valve problem, as they'd been aiming to rule out, but was a small hole in the heart between the chambers. It's congenital.

Christ sake, really?

It means that previously oxygenated blood is forced through the little hole and back into the lungs, which is inefficient as it takes the place of blood that actually needs to be oxygenated. Mine was obviously quite small (they didn't give me an actual measurement but I understand anything under 10mm is small) and they clearly weren't worried, but I guess there's a chance it could be adding to my overall fatigue and breathlessness.

'I'd leave well alone,' was the Doctor's advice, though.

So as you can see I have a nice little range of things which individually would make a person pretty tired: POTs, EDS, chronic pain, anaemia, malabsorption syndrome… and now a small ASD had joined the slumber party.

How fucking fabulous.

I'd need to really dig deep if I was going to overcome all this shit, but try I would! If I wasn't motivated enough already, looming poverty would surely incentivise me.

As Charlie gets closer to leaving full time education, I either need to get quite a lot better - or quite a lot worse…

As a low income household with a minor, we're lucky to receive tax credits and a bit of housing benefit to top up my meagre pay packet, but once Charlie is out of education I won't get those payments any more. They're to support Charlie, not me.

I knew I'd need more money coming in, even if I started to shop in Lidl instead of Tesco's, but since I was deemed too well to qualify for PIP I'd either need to get bad enough to score more points and meet the criteria, or well enough to work more hours.

I know which one I prefer, so I'm determined to help myself as much as I can.

Chapter 20

Speculate To Accumulate

There are some wonderfully knowledgeable people on Facebook, and I've recently been directed to another group for people with EDS. There's a page which lists a selection of 'tried-and-tested' supplements designed to help rebuild faulty collagen, and ease some of the other problematic symptoms EDSers have. The main list includes eight different ingredients for a better life, and people swear by it. It was designed by a rather determined mother who, along with her three daughters, are now said to be symptom-free.

I went ahead and ordered all the pills and powders from Amazon. It cost me a small fortune, but you have to speculate to accumulate, and I'm giving it a go. It takes months - up to a year, they say - to know if it's working. But with any luck, the polysaccharide will help the joint hypermobility and POTs symptoms, the D Ribose will help the chronic fatigue, the PQQ will help my bowel and bladder problems...

I won't go into too much detail in case you're not interested - if you are you can Facebook search The Cusack Protocol and all the information will be there, along with the knowledgeable community to answer any questions you might have. I'm in no way affiliated with these guys and I honestly can't even personally say if it works yet, but I'm open-minded, and a little hopeful.

I can't say that I was able to stop looking for answers after my neighbour gave me crystal healing and spoke to the angels for me, so I'm happy to try something else...

And while I wait for miracles, I'm still doing my exercises.

I have my doubts about what good they're doing as I seem to be in worse pain every day, but maybe it's something I just need to push through. I know Chris explained that I shouldn't fear the pain explaining, *'Just because you have a headache it doesn't necessarily mean there's something awful going on in your head,'* and said that I should just take the painkillers and keep going. I don't think he actually said the words *'no gain without pain'* but it was clearly inferred.

I'm not sure he likes me very much!

He gave me a leaflet printed by the NHS, entitled 'A Guide to Helping You Understand Persistent Pain and Its Causes'. Among other things it had diagrams showing the cycle between pain, reduced activity, increased joint stiffness and feeling low/reduced fitness. He sat next to me, shoulders touching on the edge of the treatment bed that my feet were dangling off (he could reach the floor), and drew a little person in the middle of the pain-cycle diagram.

'That's you!' he said.

Ahhh, that grin will end me.

He then drew a key next to the 'pain' circle and wrote 'analgesics' next to it, glancing down at me to check I was following.

He then drew a door next to 'reduced activity', which the 'analgesic key' would of course open, and then wrote 'physical exercise' in the open doorway. It was all very motivational, but it didn't make dealing with today's pain any easier.

I'm not a total wimp... when I broke my wrist I didn't shout, swear or cry, I just found Charlie's dad and said, *'Would you mind driving me to A&E please, I've broken my wrist.'*

Same when I sliced into my finger deep enough to see the bone - I'd dripped a trail blood all the way in from the garden and calmly said *'Sorry, I need another lift to A&E, please.'*

Oh and of course I've given birth without an epidural (the anaesthetist was too busy) so I think I have a reasonable pain threshold.

I just wish the current pain would back the hell off a bit.

Chapter 21

Life's A Beach

I've been taking the Midodrine for quite a while now. I don't particularly enjoy the fact that it makes me feel like I have a head full of nits (an itchy scalp is a common, if unusual side effect) especially given that I work in a school and an actual head full of nits is a genuine occupational hazard. I'm often checking... But besides that, there are no nasty side effects and I think it's helping.

Hu-flippin-ray!

I've also kept up with the expensive supplements and, dare I say it, I think I have a touch more energy! I'm a bit scared to push it too much in case I crash (it can be a bit boom or bust with chronic fatigue) but I'm gradually building up my confidence. If I can keep this up it'll be very good news indeed.

So, I've been trying to take little strolls with Lillie at least once a week over the school holidays. It's a bit hilly walking down towards the beach from home, so even though it's only about a mile away I take the car as far as the car park and walk from there. It's such a lovely beach I can't believe I've only made it down here about a dozen times in the four years I've lived here! It's good to give my eyes a chance to focus on something further away than the TV in my lounge.

It's a beach made of large, smooth pebbles and the sea makes quite a din as the tide rolls in.

Red clay cliffs rise up at either end of the beach, a bit like the ones in the TV show Broadchurch, and pastel-coloured beach huts line the promenade.

The next town along has a vast sandy beach and is more touristy, with an arcade, a big wheel and a small bowling alley - but our beach is unspoiled by this commercialism because most people like to holiday where they can make sandcastles.

I can't manage to walk along the uneven pebbles yet, maybe one day, but there's a flat footpath running from the car park all the way to the ice cream shop at the other end, which marks the start of the old high street with its charity shops and gift shops. It's a small town with a population of only about 6,000 people (and about 20,000 seagulls - not my favourite aspect of seaside living), although that probably at least doubles in the summer months. We don't mind sharing our lovely seaside, though.

Now, while all of this is quite interesting and should've been enough to fill me with immense happiness, there was another happy sight at the beach today...

◆

I've been signed off from the Wellbeing Hub. I was allowed to stay on their list for a few months and was shown how to work on all the parts of the little scribbled in 'me' on Chris's clipboard, so it's now down to me to keep it up. I can go back if a new problem arises but it's only fair to give someone else a chance to get off the waiting list.

I hadn't seen Chris for, oh… maybe a few weeks now? Until I got a tap on the shoulder as I was on my way back to the car.

'Lizzy! It's great to see you doing so well!'

Chris was out for a serious-looking run, putting me totally to shame for slowly pootling along with a little help from Lillie, who was pulling me onwards with her lead. Realising we'd stopped to speak to somebody, she jumped all over him with a great excitement usually reserved only for Kevin the vet.

'Hey Lillie, I bet you're pleased your mum is doing so well too!' he said.

Her mum was wishing she'd bothered to straighten her hair and not just stick it in a ponytail thinking 'nobody will see me, anyway' but we'll let that go.

'I knew you brought the down dog here some Sunday afternoons so I wondered if I'd bump into you,' he said.

He did??

'I was wondering how you've been getting on. I know it was still a struggle to get through the exercises when we signed you off, but have you managed to keep them going?' he asked, managing not to sound like a nag.

I didn't ask *'you were wondering about me?'*

Instead I replied, 'Yes, it's going OK thanks. I had to lay off the leg lift for a few days because it was making my eyes leak, but I started again a couple of days ago and it's not so bad.'

'That bad eh? Sorry it's tough, but if you can keep it going I hope it'll start getting easier soon,' he said.

'Yeah I'll persevere. Anyway, you're out for a run? That explains how you stay so fit!'

Shit, did that sound lechy?

'Yeah I do triathlons. Just for fun, I'm not that competitive, but it keeps me fit and busy.'

Hmmm no wife to keep you busy then??

'Oh, nice!'

He grinned as if to say *'yeah I know I'm showing off when you have problems...'* but I guess he knows I'm not the type to think he's being judgy or anything.

As if reading the direction my mind had gone in he said, 'You know I think you're pretty brave, Lizzy?'

'Ah, behave, I'm not brave! Brave is volunteering to go off and fight for your country. I didn't volunteer to be sick for the greater good, I just didn't have a choice!' I said.

'OK, but how you deal with it is. You never dropped the smile from your face even when I knew you were really hurting. And look at you now, out and about with Lillie even though your fainting made you reluctant to go out much for a few years. That's brave, isn't it?' he asked.

Oh god, I hate people being nice to me like this - I never know how to react. Odd child that I was, I even used to dislike my own birthday when I was growing up.

I hated being the center of attention and even got really awkward about being given presents because I was shy about saying thank you. I know, freak... So I won't lie, I was starting to squirm.

'Are you going this way? I'll walk with you a bit. I need to cool down after my run,' he said, setting off in the direction I'd been strolling.

'Um, yeah. OK.'

He stroked down his moderately hipster beard then raked back his hair with his hand and we started to head towards the car park. He was probably feeling a bit sweaty after his run, but if I didn't know any better I might think this mirrored my own nervous gesture of hooking my hair behind my ear. (Not the actual beard-smoothing, of course).

He shortened his stride to keep down with me (not sure if that's a saying but the point being I couldn't keep up with him), and as we fell into step over an awkward silence he smiled down at me. When I'd seen him at the Hub one of us had usually been lying down - first him to demonstrate and then me to practice, and it struck me that he was taller (or I was shorter) than I'd really realised.

If I wasn't careful I'd get a pain in my neck and have to make another appointment.

'So, I hope you don't think I'm being creepy, but I was wondering if you'd like to take my mobile number. In case you have any problems with your exercises. You could, you know, call me if you want?' he said, more tentatively than I was used to seeing him.

Oh??

He laughed then and said, 'My God, do you know how hard it is to do this these days? It's scary offering someone your phone number! I couldn't do it while I was at work, I could have got fired, but now you're not a patient, I just thought…'

Oh!!

I mean, he was right of course. #metoo had made it impossible for modern men - and I say for 'men' because they would be much less likely to complain about sexism should a woman ask them out instead. I'm not sure that we have won the equality that generations of women may have dreamt of. Instead we seem have a strange kind of reversal, and men have become somewhat downtrodden by new rules about what's considered acceptable behaviour.

There was a story recently about a delivery guy who was sacked for texting one of his regulars to ask her out. He'd got her number from her account, which was a data breach, and asking her out counted as harassment so he was arrested and cautioned. In the old days people might have thought this was romantic, after all we were brought up daydreaming about the Milk Tray man climbing into our bedroom windows to leave us a box of chocolates on our dressing table…

Let's face it; Richard Gere's Pretty Woman would never have been made given today's attitude, which makes me wonder why Fifty Shades met with such popular approval. Had Mr Grey been a bin man instead of a millionaire, I'm sure it would've been a darker story about stalking…

It's no wonder people have to meet online these days; almost anything else is a potentially chargeable offence. Bloody shame! I may have encountered some weirdos in my time, but isn't it a bit sad that there's no romance anymore?

I fear for Charlie's generation…

Anyway, of course I took his phone number and thanked him, feeling that he'd been rather brave to offer it to me.

We got to my car before the ticket ran out, and he held the door open for me while I loaded the dog in. The other good thing about this beach is that I don't end up with a ton of sand left on the back seat.

I'm not good at reading cues and I was still a bit confused about what had just happened but I said, *'It was nice to see you, have a good run back!'* and he closed the door for me then stood and waved as I pulled away.

I'm not sure if he knows what he's doing with that big grin - do you think somebody once told him it makes him irresistible, so he uses it on purpose as a weapon?

Chapter 22

A Nice Problem To Have

So, anyway. That happened.

'Good God, talk about ridiculously incompatible!' I said to the girls.

'In one corner you have a fit, good looking bloke, who chooses to take on triathlons - for fun - and in the other there's me, who struggles to get off the sofa! What on earth would he see in me!? Surely he's just being kind by offering me help if I need it, now I'm not on the list for the Hub. It's probably *charity,*' I said.

'Oh my God are you blind as well as crippled!?' blurted Kay. I love that she takes the piss - it's so much better than people who tread carefully in case they hurt my feelings. I'm not dying, I can take a joke.

'Look, he went out running at the time and place he thought he'd bump into you. Are you telling me that doesn't mean anything?' suggested Elle.

Hmm. I had wondered about that. Was it a one off coincidence, or had he been running here for weeks just in case? I wasn't about to ask him, that's for sure.

'I can't tell what he's hiding under that beard and I might be way too old for him!' I said. This was a genuine concern, actually. I'm 48 now (although I feel more like 88) and he might think that was grossly old!

'Didn't he get you to confirm your address and date of birth at your first appointment?' reminded Elle.

I face-palmed my response. Of course, they always check they have the correct patient in front of them by checking their personal details and yes, he'd read out my date of birth.

'Well then, he knows! He must be around the same age. Either that, or he doesn't care!' insisted Elle.

Huh. But what to do?

Do I like him? Yes, I think so.

We've only really talked about what I was at the Hub for, and not much else, so I didn't really know anything about him. But he *seemed* really nice.

Did I fancy him? Well, yes.

He was obviously in good shape (unlike me) and I didn't mind the hipster beard. He had nice brown eyes that crinkled when he smiled - which he did quite a lot.

But so what? Nothing would ever come of it. He might be a good physio but even he would never get me well enough to go running with him. Our lives are completely incompatible.

He probably did things like *clean eating* too.

Even though I've been veggie for about 30 years I certainly wasn't virtuous. I'd turned veggie by accident when I started to get over Glandular Fever when I was 16. I'd been living off cold rice pudding from a tin for weeks - it went down without hurting my throat too much and had just about enough substance to keep me from starving.

I'd eventually come around to the idea of actual food again, but found that I'd become squeamish about what I could face trying. Mum suggested everything she could think of and when she asked me, 'What about some nice minced beef?' I suddenly felt pukey.

'Urgh that's bloody, dead stuff!'

'Prawn cocktail?' (This had been our special-occasion treat as was common in the 80s).

'Urgh, no thanks - it smells fishy!'

For some reason thinking about food in a fresh light, as opposed to just continuing to eat what I'd been given as a kid, made my squeamish threshold rather sensitive. I don't know how I ever stomached liver and onions – a midweek staple up until then. Most people had 'a line', whether it be that they eat cow but not horse, or sheep but not dog… or that they'd eat steak but not brain. But to me it suddenly all seemed equally gross.

I wouldn't lick a live animal so I certainly didn't want to eat dead ones!

It wasn't easy to be veggie in those days, either - you had to phone ahead to the pub and ask if the chef would be willing to make you an omelette, but I never managed to eat meat again. Mad cow disease probably put the final nail in that particular coffin.

But I wasn't a healthy-eater. I was too knackered and skint to only eat an organic, plant based diet.

I'd tried Ella's cookbook but the things I made didn't taste good, and the ingredients cost a fortune so I went back to snacking on kit-kats.

I'm sure a health conscious - triathlete - physio would not approve of my junk diet.

◆

Anyway, I simply didn't have the nerve to phone or text the mobile number Chris had given to me. I didn't need any particular help with my exercises, and that was why he said to call, so I was worried I'd make a fool of myself if I got in touch without that excuse.

What I did do, rather bravely I thought, was to take the dog out at the same time the next Sunday.

Just, you know, to see....

Chapter 23

Sunday, Sunday Here Again, Tidy Attire

(To quote Blur's early 1990s song).

I straightened my hair and put some makeup on before I went out this time. I even spritzed my signature Boss Orange on - I would usually think it was a waste of good perfume if I was just walking the dog, but you know...

I didn't go so far as to shave my legs, even if I did bump into Chris my leg stubble wouldn't be exposed in my skinny jeans, and I had to preserve some energy for smiling. I'd had a good lie-in, but now Lillie had brought me her lead and was dancing around with it telling me she wanted to go out. She's not that daft after all - she'd learned the new Sunday afternoon routine fast enough.

I felt a bit nervous!

What the hell was I doing?

I parked up and we set off along the level path. I'd almost got to the town end when I felt a tap on my shoulder.

Gulp.

'Hi Lizzy!'

Oh.

It was Kevin.

'Hiiii Lillieeee… I've missed you! Yes hi, hi!' he said, bending down to fuss Lillie who was beside herself! I let him say hi to Lillie for a while, and lo and behold, who should walk past eating an ice cream?

Allotment man.

At least he's not dead; I could stop worrying about him now.

This was all starting to feel like a weird dream. All I needed was PB and Dickhead to walk past and I'd feel like Scrooge being shown his past lives so he'd realise what a git he'd been.

What was the message here, I wondered?

I let my eyes return to Kevin who seemed reluctant to let Lillie go, and just as he was tearing himself away I saw a blur rush past. I was starting to feel a bit dizzy with all this to and froing when the blur turned around and started jogging backwards, but still away from me.

Seeing that Kevin had now walked off in the other direction, Chris laser-beamed me with his disarming grin and ran forwards again, arriving back to where I was standing and wondering who might be teleported into my weird day next.

'I thought you had company so I left you to it,' panted Chris.

'Oh no, that was Lillie's vet. He just stopped to say hello to her,' I told him.

Which prompted him to say hi to her too. He didn't mention the fact that I hadn't got in touch.

'So how's it going? Still got a pain in the arse?' he laughed.

'Yes!' I play-punched his arm. It wouldn't exactly be a hard punch would it, not with my busted shoulder. 'And I blame you, you know!'

'Yeah I know, sorry. So, would you let me buy you a coffee to make up for it?' he asked.

He did that thing where he raked his hand through his hair again - maybe it was nerves after all. He gestured to the little hut down on the beach where you could get coffee and cake and said, 'Dogs are allowed on that bit of the beach, I checked.'

He'd checked.

They had a few tables laid out on a flat terraced area and we could see one was free. We had to go down a few steps as the path was higher than the beach in this part - he had half an eye on me as we went down, as if checking I was managing OK, but I didn't huff, puff or swear about using them! *See I've been doing my homework!*

As he put two steaming mugs of coffee down on the table, checking it wouldn't wobble as he did, he asked 'How's Charlie?'

So, he had remembered I had a son. Good. It came up at my first appointment when Chris had asked if there was anyone else at home. They always ask that, half checking whether there's someone to help you and half checking what your responsibilities are, I guess.

'Yeah he's good thanks. He's gone to the cinema with his friends.'

'Oh there must be something teen-friendly on, my son went yesterday!'

Huh. So he has a family....

'He stays with me on alternate weekends. It's his weakened to stay here but he's 17 now so he's off doing his own thing most of the time. He comes out on the bike with me now and then, but he's not that bothered these days,' he said, passing me my mug of coffee.

Oh, a son, but maybe not a family.

And so we chatted about our kids and the difficult time they have with exams these days, and the scary shit parents go through when they start to learn to drive.

It turns out Chris had always been a bit of a runner, but he took up triathlons when he got divorced to fill the time when his son was with his mum. He was closer in age than I thought - he was just 2 years younger than me in birth years, although in physical health years there was at least half a century between us. But he was easy to talk to, and he already knew about my issues so I didn't have to do the dreaded explaining.

'I do admire you Lizzy. You're such a positive person,' he said.

Oh, cringe time.

'I am a positive person - there's a lot to be positive about! I separated my mental wellbeing from my physical health a long time ago and I don't let it make me sad. I could live without it, but it's nothing to be sad about,' I said, meaning every word.

'I know people who've had years of cognitive behaviour therapy to learn how to live with chronic pain and you managed to find a way through it all on your own. I know you didn't get diagnosed for years, so you didn't get the support you deserved, but you still didn't let it get you down. You should be proud of yourself,' he said.

'I always looked forward to you coming in because you were so cheerful. You appreciated the help, listened to the advice, and you did your exercises. Not every patient is so nice to treat! There are some who get angry with us because they've had to wait for a while before we could fit them in, and they haven't got half the problems you have to put up with. Then there are the ones who complain about not getting better but you just know they're not doing the exercises. They pretend they are, but we can tell when people aren't trying to help themselves.'

'You really tried though. I know you'll never cure your problems but you're so determined not to let them steal your life!' he said.

He looked at me like he was so proud... I felt awkward!

I changed the subject - that was quite enough talking about me.

We soon found ourselves talking about what TV and films we liked, what music we grew up with, our favourite food (he wasn't a food saint after all, which was a relief) and suddenly Chris stopped talking, and looked into my eyes with that beaming grin on his face again.

'You do realise we've just had our first date?' he said.

Holy Fuck - *Kay will pee her pants.*

'Have we?' I asked, eyes wide in an *are you teasing me?* query.

'Well, it felt like a date to me. I didn't want to ask you out for dinner because you'd told me that eating out sometimes brought on your POTs symptoms and I didn't want you to worry. I just hoped that if I bumped into you down here you'd let me buy you a coffee so we could get to know each other a bit in a more relaxed way,' he said.

He had a bit of a *'shit, I hope this is OK'*, look on his face (it was).

He smoothed down his beard again, which I now noticed had one or two touches of grey in it, and carried on, 'You said you felt better out in the fresh air than in stuffy pubs, so I thought this was a perfect spot.'

I wanted to reassure him that it was indeed a perfect spot and to thank him for being so thoughtful, but I was actually genuinely lost for words for a minute. I filled the pause by bending down and fussing Lillie, telling her she was a good *girl since* she'd sat nicely under the table while we had our second coffee.

'So, what do you say to a second date?'

'I don't want to be pushy and please, please say no if you're not interested. I promise I'll leave you alone! But if you'd like to, maybe we could meet here again next week? If you feel up to it that is?' Chris asked.

'I'd like that,' I managed to reply, and was rewarded with his look of relief - possibly that I wouldn't report him for stalking. This, of course, turned into that boyish grin again a second later.

We left together and he put a gentle hand in the middle of my back as we climbed the steps. Maybe he was worried that my dodgy right leg would give out on me. It felt nice.

I tried not to think he must feel like he's helping his granny up the steps, and at least he didn't say *'mind how you go,'* like I would if it was my 82 year old mum, but it reminded me that he knew I was a bit broken.

I dwelled on this when I got home and part of me worried that I might be a bit of a *project.* Was it the fact that I was a bit busted that made me interesting to somebody who's learned about fixing people?

'Don't be a daft cow,' Kay said, when I asked this question out loud.

Elle added 'I'm sure he's not attracted to you because of your problems. It's just that he's attracted to you despite them because he's not scared of them. He knows you manage OK and you're still you - he just doesn't really see the other stuff, same as we don't.'

'Trust me, it's *you*, our lovely friend that he's interested in!' said Kay.

She did go on to discuss how some of my problems might have to be negotiated if we took things further and then she recounted a story she'd seen on *Sex Sent Me To The E.R*, which she could barely finish between fits of giggles, but you don't need to know about that!

I couldn't help but think about how far apart our lives were though. I've always struggled to keep up - what chance did I have of keeping up with a sodding triathlete?

Chapter 24

The Sunny Side

'Who says you have to keep up?' asked Elle.

'He hasn't asked you to meet up and go running, he's invited you to meet for coffee at a picnic table!'

Trust Elle and her good points to take the wind out of my arguments. She was right about that, of course.

'You said yourself you're staying awake a bit more at the weekends now too, maybe you'll start to want more company if you're not sleeping your days away so much.'

'What've you got to lose? I can tell you're secretly interested by the glint in your eyes that you're trying to ignore. We can see it, Lizzy! You're starting to want this, you just have to let go of the fear. Don't let your past determine your future,' said Kay, who looked to Elle for approval in a *see, I can be wise too* way.

I'd been pretty good at recalling the phrase *'don't look back, you're not going that way,'* but I suppose I was even more cautious about attempting to date after the Dickhead debacle. I had to take a breath and remind myself of another comment that had always stuck with me.

As a young girl I was walking to school with mum and I was totally amazed when we turned a corner to see that one side of the street was being pelted with heavy rain, but by crossing over the road we were walking in the sunshine.

I clearly remember mum saying *'the rain has to end somewhere,'* and thinking that was *really bloody profound.*

Well maybe she's right; I need to remember to walk on the bright side of life.

So, I've given Chris my mobile number. It seems sensible in case he's ever unable to come out as arranged, so he'd be able to let me know and not just stand me up. He could probably have got the number from my file at work, but I didn't want him getting into trouble under the complicated new GDPR rules - and I figured if things went tits up I could always change my number.

He's sent me a few texts, just a few words here and there. Nothing demanding, and no requests for nudes, so I'm gaining confidence that he's as genuine as he seems.

He asked how I would feel about a pub beer garden instead of the beach hut cafe for a change, so we'd still be outside (so I'd be less likely to feel POTsy), and the dog could still come. He was happy that she gave me the motivation to get out a bit these days so he didn't want to leave her out. That sounded OK to me, and meant we could have proper food, which would save me from having to bother later.

The pub nearest the beach gets a bit busy on a Sunday, but we found a spot and I was reminded how much easier it is to do stuff when you have a helpful adult around, as he sat me down and suggested I stay with the dog while he went in to order.

Someone offering to do the hard bits made this a much more pleasurable experience.

When I'd been married I had tried to do my share, not expecting it to be a male role, but this wasn't a gender issue - it was just Chris quietly working around my challenges with me.

This was our third date (if we include the one I hadn't realised was a date at all) which meant that the conversation was becoming a bit more personal. I suppose at some point we were bound to want to get to know a bit more about each other. Some of the meaty stuff…

Having explained in passing that we were each divorced, we delved a little deeper in to the when and why. We also started to discuss what we'd each done with our lives since, although my divorce was more ancient history than his was, and I vaguely explained about PB and Dickhead.

'No dates since? It's been a while then. Not tempted to join Tinder?' he asked.

'Absolutely not!' I replied 'Did you?'

'Yeah I admit I tried it for a few weeks, but I hated it. First off, nobody looks like their photos! They Photoshop them to death or use really old ones, which I will never understand because that pretense is blown as soon as you meet up. Secondly, the people I met were all vacuous - I didn't find one genuine person looking for a good old-fashioned relationship,' he said, confirming my view that it was a young person's game.

'I work full time, I have responsibilities even if my lad is off to Uni soon, and I've been married. I'm just not in the market for one night stands with people that have no conversation,' he told me.

He must've read my mind because he sort-of answered one of my concerns without me even having to raise it. I was picking at the little splinters of wood on the table with my finger nail. Sometimes I find direct eye contact a bit intense and when conversations get a bit *real* I notice the discomfort even more. I'd never quite lost my shyness.

'I stopped looking ages ago and decided I was happy enough on my own. I have my sports to keep me busy and a few good mates so I can't say I'm exactly lonely. But then you came along and I thought, 'Here's a person worth getting to know better!' And I know what you're going to ask me next!' he said.

I looked up as if to say 'I'm not sure you do,' but he was already proving me wrong. 'You want to know whether your EDS and POTs problems bother me?' he said beaming that dangerous smile back at me.

'Ok, yes I suppose I have been wondering about that. I'm hardly able to meet you half way with your hobbies - I'll never be up to going running, I fall off bikes, and you'll *never* get me sea swimming! I don't travel abroad these days, I sleep more than your average person, and I've got no interest in going to things like concerts or festivals,' I pointed out.

I wasn't trying to put myself down or warn him off as much as make sure he knew what he was getting into.

'I'm doing better than I was this time last year, but these aren't problems that will ever go away. I'd say that makes me a pretty dull prospect!' I said.

'Do you not see your good points, Lizzy?' he asked.

'All of what you just said is just background noise - it's not who you are. You're a good person, you're smart and bright, you're always smiling, and you've proven that you're determined not to be beaten by life. There's a lot to admire about you!' he said.

Christ on a bike this was getting embarrassing now.

I was letting Lillie take the heat out of the situation, hoping it would do the same for my cheeks, by reaching down to feed her a sliver of apple from my ploughman's lunch. (Sorry Kevin I know she's on a controlled diet, but she's being so good!).

'Maybe you need to think about it from my perspective for a minute,' he said. 'What do you think I would look for in a relationship?'

I wasn't meaning to be awkward but I didn't exactly have an answer to this, so I grinned back and shrugged, which he rightly took to mean, *'Go on then, tell me...'*

'I'm middle-aged, my beard is going grey (he said with that grin again, as if to say *what can you do?*), I'm busy with work - which I enjoy. I own my own house, I cook and clean for myself, I certainly don't need somebody to look after me...'

OK, this was all fair.

'My sports are my wind-down time and to be honest I like doing them on my own. I would never expect a future girlfriend to want to come running with me and that's fine - it's my 'me time' anyway, I suppose.'

So, that's all sounding okay, right?

'There's only one thing missing in my life, if anything, and that's having somebody worth coming home to. When I'm done with work and my sports it would be nice to have someone to chat to when I get back in the house, because there's no denying it feels quite empty sometimes,' he said.

I couldn't fault his willingness to open up, could I?

'Sure I can put the TV on, but there's nobody to cuddle up to when I take time out to watch a film!' he said.

'You can think about the ways we might seem incompatible, but if things go well for us I think we're actually more compatible than you realise,' he insisted.

'I suppose when you meet somebody as an adult it's very different than when you start a relationship as teenagers,' I conceded.

'I know when I met Charlie's dad we were in such a hurry all the time - we hurried to live together, we hurried to buy a house. We lived in each other's pockets and if we weren't at work, we were together. We did everything as a couple. I suppose by our age we know ourselves better and have got used to some independence, so that's not how it has to work,' I said.

'Exactly! So think about it – you'd get your quiet time and I wouldn't have somebody complaining that I wasn't being attentive enough! Then after you've had your peace and quiet and I'm done in from my run, we'd maybe both be ready to cuddle up in front of the TV together?' he said, painting a rather nice picture.

'I understand your issues, so they wouldn't worry or frustrate me, and anyway I just don't see them really. We're sitting here talking like two perfectly normal human beings, aren't we?' he grinned.

'Did you just call me *normal*? How dare you!' I teased.

Our plates were being cleared and we started to get up to make way for a family who were looking around hoping for an empty spot. Chris motioned to them that we were leaving so they could start to make their way over, and then he untied Lillie's lead, which he held onto as we left.

What happened next was perfectly natural, but it gave me such a jolt I almost stopped breathing. I'd managed to stay on my feet for our easy-going dates so far, and I didn't want to ruin things now, so I remembered to breathe out...

As Chris held onto Lillie's lead with one hand, he gently took mine with the other.

It's been *forever* since anybody had held my hand, and the last time had been the soft little hand of nine year old Charlie, before he got far too old for that nonsense.

Chris' much larger, warm, *manly* hand holding mine was such a strange feeling, it took me a moment to calm down the fluttering butterflies in my chest. And this time I couldn't blame the small hole in my heart.

Now, I know many of today's kids jump into bed on their first Tinder date (not that I'm judging) and here I was getting over excited about hand-holding on our third, but what can I say? It's been a while!

He glanced down at me, his eyelashes casting a little shadow under his eyes, as if to check that I was OK with this development. I was probably hard to read because while it was very much OK, for a moment I wasn't sure that *I* was, but the heart flutters were fleeting and I soon realised it was actually *really nice.*

'I know we're still just getting to know each other and we don't know what's around the corner. There could be a lot of reasons we don't end up getting on as well as I hope we will, but your health problems won't be the reason. We can take it slowly. We might not be getting any younger, (he paused to flash his *what the hell does that matter* smile) but there's no reason to rush into anything,' he said reassuringly.

'No, I agree. I'd always been in a rush to reach the next milestone, whether that was buying a house at 19, or aiming for the next promotion. But one thing being a bit poorly has taught me is how to slow down,' I told him.

'Everybody is rushing through life and all I hear from most people I know is how terribly busy they are. I've found a way to get everything done that needs doing, even if not to the show-home standards I used to aim for, but I still have loads of down time,' I said.

'I can categorically state that I am never really busy, and I don't think I've *rushed* since about 1999! I've learned that doing what I like, even if that's just sitting in the garden and reading a book, isn't wasting time - it's *taking* time,' I said as I watched the ferry full of tourists pass by.

'So, we don't have a problem. You can take time to do what you like to do, and I can take time to enjoy my sports, and in between those times we can figure out if *this* (he said lifting our joined hands a little) could make us both happy.'

As we strolled along the flat promenade towards our parked cars he paused, turned to face me and said...

'If anything it sounds to me like our differences could work for both us. We could be perfect partners.'

Epilogue

It's my 50th birthday today. I've officially outlived my dad.

The girls bought me a rather risqué zebra-print corset with a gift tag saying, 'Brace yourself!'

Kay says I need to *strap myself in* so I don't have to be too careful about my back in the bedroom, but she was worried that my usual orthopaedic back brace would be a bit of a passion-killer.

I can't think why!

I was inspecting the new wrinkles around my eyes and pulling out a stray grey hair that would not behave itself (why are they so wiry?) when Chris called up the stairs, *'Taxi's here!'*

I quickly popped on some Bare Minerals lip stain and grabbed my pashmina, knocking on Charlie's door to relay the *'taxi's here'* message that he'd have missed thanks to his noise-reducing headphones. He followed me down the stairs and we all jumped into the waiting car.

Charlie gets on pretty well with Jack, Chris' son, who said 'nice hair,' to Charlie as we squashed into the back seat.

Charlie has been growing out his fringe, and these days I can't just get the clippers out, I have to scissor-cut the top to match the Pinterest photo he showed me.

It seems to meet approval.

The boys are not too far apart in age and they're friends on Instagram and Discord, so I think they keep in touch quite a bit. We don't see much of Jack these days because he's away at Uni in Manchester, but he comes home for part of the school holidays.

The four of us are heading out for a birthday meal.

I'm not sure if it's the Cusack Protocol, or the Midodrine, the CBD oil, or the physio - or maybe it's just the love of a good man - but I'm no longer too scared to eat out.

So, we're off to the nearby Thai restaurant.

I doubt I'll order tofu green curry, there are just too many memories of the fateful day trip to London, but there will be something yummy, I'm sure.

As we arrived at The Lime Leaf, the boys went on ahead while Chris held my hand to help me out of the car. All three of them tower over me so I'm a bit outnumbered, but I love them all.

As the taxi drove away and before he opened the restaurant door (if there's a heavy-looking door Chris grabs it first, not so much out of chivalry but so I don't pull my shoulder out of the socket) he gently put a hand on my arm to stop me from walking straight past.

He quietly whispered, *'Happy birthday Lizzy,'* before planting a kiss on my lips.

'Gross,' I think I heard one of the boys say under his breath from the restaurant doorway, but it wasn't.

It *really* wasn't.

It was the perfect birthday present.

Bonus chapter

An MRI Scandal

I wrote this after discovering some worrying information about MRIs. People with chronic illness are often given MRIs as part of their diagnostic journey, and yet they are perhaps the most susceptible to the problems of toxicity that are now being acknowledged.

I deleted the following as it didn't seem to fit Lizzy's story - it sort of broke the flow, I think. I've popped it back here in case anybody wants to read it, because the problem with contrast MRIs is sadly very real. If you can be arsed, knock yourself out!

I've got a cousin, on my dad's side of the family, who recently became unwell. His mum phoned my mum a while ago asking about my dad, and why he'd died so young. I was only 16 when he died and my memory of the whole period is a bit vague, but I'd never thought that we could 'catch' what he had, so it hadn't concerned me. It wasn't the cause of my perceived hypercondria, if you're wondering.

They couldn't remember what the condition was, and they wanted to know because my cousin's Doctors were struggling to find out what was causing his symptoms.

Mum explained that dad's illness wasn't an inherited one, and went on to mention that I'd been having some problems, although she wasn't too sure what they were (since as you know I don't talk about it much, even to her), so she put my cousin in touch with me to see if there was a familial link there instead.

We talked about symptoms, but although there were some similarities, it was soon clear that we don't have the same thing.

We speak quite often now though, so something good came of it - we'd never actually met, so I've just gained a family member! And although we don't seem to have the same condition, I know what it's like to be unwell and not to know why...

His Doctors just couldn't seem to figure out what the problem was. At one point he was admitted to hospital for tests and they sat his pregnant wife down (they were expecting their second child) and told her he had Amyotrophic Lateral Sclerosis (ALS), with a life expectancy that averages about two to five years from the time of diagnosis!

It wasn't that in the end, but it really has been a dire time for their young family, and I was happy to be in touch with a listening ear.

I tell you what, though - we are not very alike! He showed me how a different attitude (and private health cover!) can make a difference. He pushed back, and he pushed back hard - a super impressive reaction to a shocking diagnosis.

He had tests upon tests, and with some fight and determination it wasn't too much longer before he got a diagnosis.

Now, I have never heard of this before - but basically he had been poisoned by Gadolinium.

I know - what the fuck is that?

No, he's not a spy and it wasn't an assassination attempt, although it might as well have been...

Before things kicked off he'd gone to his Doctor with a relatively minor complaint about his digestion. He wanted to know if perhaps he had IBS, or celiac disease, or something (or hopefully nothing) along those lines. Being covered by insurance, he soon found himself offered a range of gold-standard tests, which included a contrast MRI.

The 'contrast' they use is called Gadolinium. As a lay person, we might say we've had an MRI with 'dye' and be of the firm belief that this dye passes through our system very easily within a few hours. This is what we're told, anyway.

Gadolinium is actually a: 'silvery-white, malleable, and ductile rare earth metal'. Yes, a metal.

Metal shouldn't live in a body, we're not robots...

With great gusto he looked into this and Jesus Christ it turns out they've been pumping this shit into people of all ages for years. The worst thing is that there's plenty of evidence, easily found online, acknowledging that this stuff is not good news.

You know, we trust them don't we? We're offered tests which are bound to be safe, right? And we're handed a piece of paper with tiny writing on it at the point we're about to be tested, and we sign our consent.

But it isn't *safe*.

Over the last few months we've discovered that his sudden health problems were due to this test, which he didn't really need, causing Gadolinium Deposition Disease. We've discovered that people the world over are suffering from the effects of this toxic stuff.

I've just paused to Google it so I can explain it properly. This is what you can find online now: There is a wide spectrum of adverse effects that may occur, potentially causing toxicities and gadolinium deposition disease (GDD). Patients with GDD develop an immunologic response that is dependent on the genetic susceptibility of an individual. Symptoms include bone pain, skin and subcutaneous tissue burning pain, and various intensities of what is described as "chemo brain" or "brain fog."

Progressive thickening and discoloration of the skin and subcutaneous tissue of the distal arms and legs can occur in late stage disease. Symptoms of GDD occur within hours to days of gadolinium-based contrast agent administration.

Shit!

So, this otherwise healthy young lad went to his Doctor with tummy pains, possibly caused by something simple and easily managed, and has ended up seriously unwell thanks to one of the tests they throw around willy-nilly these days.

If you think you might've had this and want to look into it there's plenty of information online now. You could also search Facebook for Chuck and Gena Norris (yes the famous actor!) as they've been campaigning on this because Gena got sick with GDD too.

We stayed up late one night soon after we learned about this problem, writing a long and detailed letter between us over messenger, which we would address to his MP and the Health Secretary. I pulled on my old 'communications' hat, and between us we explained the problem, quoted research, and put together a letter that has, frankly, caused some mayhem.

Our NHS can be completely amazing - it's helped me and my family numerous times and I've seen nothing but good from it. But, the bigger the ship, the slower it turns and the NHS is in complete denial about this problem, determined that it doesn't exist and not even entertaining the idea of testing. But guess what - partly thanks to our letter, this issue is now being heard and they are 'discussing' it!

There's no official acknowledgement yet, that is probably still a bit of a way off and fear of compensation claims will muddy the waters, but with any luck we can get unnecessary use of this shit prevented in future so more people are not affected.

He's been interviewed by Sky News and was even prepared to pose for a 'sad face' photo for the Daily Mail if it got the message across, but it hasn't quite had to come to that.

Which is good as I did say I would have to disown him.

So, here's the thing. I have had *two* contrast MRIs.

Indeed.

Fuckadoodledoo.

The difference between us is that I don't have access to private health care - it doesn't exactly come with a part-time school job - so I can't get tested unless I pay for it myself, which I can't afford. And even if I found that I had GDD, I would not be able to afford the £5k it cost him to go and seek treatment in Holland, so there's kind of no point me getting tested anyway. Not that the treatment 100% rectifies the problem - it just 'takes the edge off' by removing some of the heavy metal. It'll always be stuck in his body, which is scary shit.

There are of course many people who have MRIs who won't have this problem. They may retain the stuff, as it appears that everybody does, but the current information suggests there may be a genetic predisposition to GDD after a contrast MRI. So people with wonky genes may develop problems, and given that we are related, this could potentially mean the downturn in my health could have some link to the MRIs I had, too.

But, unless the NHS takes this problem seriously, accepts responsibility and starts testing, then I will never know.

There's a legal case building momentum and I may be able to join it as some stage, as a potential 'victim', which would open up access to treatment I guess. At that point I suppose I would bite the bullet and stick the cost of a test on my credit card…

Christ alive.

There's one thing I can do without getting further into debt though. That is to take a leaf out of his book and fight a bit harder for my own answers. Perhaps I've been too accepting, and gone away to struggle on my own, fearful of being a burden...

About the writer

I say 'writer' rather than author because while Lizzy is made up, much of what she experiences is based on my life. Particularly the illness-related bits.

I really am a divorcee, fast-approaching 50, and I really do have an amazing son, soon to turn 15 years old.

Sadly Lizzy's happy ending is pure fantasy but it was fun to write!

I really do have Ehlers Danlos Syndrome (hEDS) and POTs, so Lizzy's journey to find out why she kept fainting was quite close to the truth. As was the timeframe for finally getting diagnosed, first of POTs at age 38, and finally of EDS at 47.

I apologise if anybody is offended by the sweary bits!

Honestly, I don't really swear in real life (I might be middle-aged but mum would still clip me around the ear) but my alter-ego obviously needs her mouth washing out with soap.

The reason I *allowed* this, is that I hate when people treat poorly people as if they're delicate flowers. We're real people, and we come in all sorts of packages, and I wanted Lizzy to be a bit robust. I didn't want people to feel sorry for her, but to laugh with her. Swearing a bit seemed to suit her.

The enlightened among you will know that EDS is a connective-tissue disorder, and the playful title nods at the various braces and supports EDSers use to hold themselves together. I personally have a rather nice collection of supporting paraphernalia including a back brace, compression garments for my hips, wrist supports, ankle supports, thumb support, knee braces and of course tape...

Sadly none of them are as sexy as the zebra print corset on the cover.

EDSers will know that the zebra is 'our' symbol so I had to build that into the cover design give you a hint.

I've started a Facebook page, so I can point people to various resources should they identify with Lizzy's problems. You can find it here:
https://www.facebook.com/Brace-Yourself-254343568532522/

I'm on twitter too, learning more about #amwriting every day, thanks to some helpful bloggers. I might've got the bug, you see, if only I could come up with another storyline... https://twitter.com/BraceyourselfN

Why The Zebra?

This is from https://www.ehlers-danlos.org

"When you hear the sound of hooves, think horses, not zebras."

This phrase is taught to medical students throughout their training.

In medicine, the term "zebra" is used in reference to a rare disease or condition. Doctors are taught to assume that the simplest explanation is usually correct to avoid patients being misdiagnosed with rare illnesses. Doctors learn to expect common conditions.

But many medical professionals seem to forget that "zebras" DO exist and so getting a diagnosis and treatment can be more difficult for sufferers of rare conditions. Ehlers-Danlos syndrome is considered a rare condition and so EDS sufferers are known as medical zebras. This identity has now been adopted across the world through social media to help bring our community together.

For anybody who's interested, here's my current collection of issues:

Ehlers Danlos Syndrome (hEDS), POT syndrome, scoliosis/ankylosing spondylitis, sciatica, piriformis syndrome, possible CCI & definite TMJ (which both come with migraines), MCAS (hence the sun allergy, and problems tolerating anaesthetics), complex regional pain syndrome, carpal tunnel syndrome, malabsorption syndrome, pernicious anaemia, small atrial septal defect, chronic fatigue syndrome, inflammatory bowel syndrome...

and yesterday I chipped a nail ;)

A word about Fibromyalgia - I know many people say that they have hEDS *and* fibro but I suspect in my case it was a misdiagnosis - an earlier attempt to find a label, which I think EDS supersedes. I've dropped fibro from my list! It is in Lizzy's story because it was a part of the journey...

I am yet to be tested for GDD, we'll see, eh?

Dedications

Huge thanks to K & L, my real school-gate friends whose roles in my life are much more significant than Lizzy lets on. I don't live near them any more – I met them when we lived in Hampshire and I now live back in sunny Devon... and I miss you!

A special thanks to A my real, and really amazing sister.

I actually have 3 lovely sisters but A in particular, due mainly to circumstance as we worked at the same place for many years, has really always been there for me.

Of course thanks to my wonderful mum, of 'bruised bones' fame, who continues to support all 4 of us girls. We'd be lost without you, mum.

A quick note on typos: I'm sorry if I missed any fat-finger mistakes. Let me know and I'll correct them!

And finally to you. Yes, you!

Thank you SO MUCH for reading Brace Yourself! At the time of self-publishing I have no idea whether it's just self-indulgent twaddle, or if there's an audience for Lizzy's story, so thank you so much if you read it! To once again borrow Lizzy's words, *'It's f***ing marvellous!'*

I hope you think Lizzy would make a nice friend! She's been mine while writing her story, anyway.

Gentle hugs xxx

Made in the USA
Coppell, TX
19 July 2020